MAURICE

A SMALLTOWN, ROMANTIC SUSPENSE

BAYOU BROTHERHOOD PROTECTORS
BOOK NINE

ELLE JAMES

TWISTED PAGE INC

Dedicated to my editor who makes my words shine and to my personal assistant for catching the typos and missing words and for working with me on tight deadlines!
Love you both!
Elle James

AUTHOR'S NOTE

Bayou Brotherhood Protectors
Remy (#1)
Gerard (#2)
Lucas (#3)
Beau (#4)
Rafael (#5)
Valentin (#6)
Landry (#7)
Simon (#8)
Maurice (#9)
Xavier (#10)
Jacques (#11)
Papa Noel (#12)

Visit ellejames.com for more titles and release dates
Join her newsletter at
https://ellejames.com/contact/

MAURICE

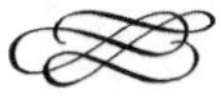

BAYOU BROTHERHOOD
PROTECTORS BOOK # 9

New York Times & *USA Today*
Bestselling Author

ELLE JAMES

PROLOGUE

FOUR YEARS AGO...

Afghanistan

"HEY, MO," Bryce Collins's voice sounded in Navy SEAL Maurice Boucher's ear. "Did you ask her?"

Maurice, aka Mo, stood with his M4A1 rifle with its sound suppressor aimed at the alley ahead of him as Perez leap-frogged forward to the corner of the next building. "Yeah."

"And?" Collins prompted.

"And we're in the middle of a mission," Maurice reminded him.

"Was it yes or no?" Rusty jumped into the conversation.

"You're supposed to have Scott's six," Maurice stalled.

"I've got Scott," Rusty assured him. "Did you get the girl?"

Maurice focused his night-vision goggles on the green silhouette of Perez and the shadows ahead of the man. "She said yes."

"Well, damn," Collins whispered. "Another hot medic taken out of the dating pool."

"We're not dating," Maurice said. "You know it's strictly forbidden in theater."

"Fraternization...blah...blah...blah," Rusty said. "Like it doesn't happen."

"Don't know why she chose you when she could've had me," Jason Tingle said.

"It's probably his Cajun accent," Collins said. "Girls like an accent."

"I got an accent," Ray Scott said. "She didn't pick me."

"She couldn't understand you," Rusty said. "What exactly are you saying when you say you 'Pawk ya caw'?"

"Better than what all you Texans are constantly spewing," Scott fired back. "It's not even a word."

"And pawk is?" Rusty countered.

"Bogey on the rooftop, my two o'clock," Perez reported.

All chitchat ceased as the SEAL team moved into the small Afghan village. Intel had it that a Taliban held two US Army soldiers in a building near the center of town. The two men were the sole survivors of a supply convoy that had hit an IED en route to a forward operating base.

The SEAL team's mission was to find the building, extract the soldiers and take out as many Taliban as possible.

They'd split up, entering the village from different directions, moving in simultaneously. The idea was to get in and out as quietly as possible to avoid waking villagers, thus minimizing chaos and collateral damage.

Perez waved Maurice forward while he pointed his rifle ahead.

Maurice joined Perez at the corner of the building and stared up at the rooftop.

A dark silhouette of a man's head and shoulders appeared. As he turned, Maurice saw that the man carried a rifle.

"Take him," Maurice said.

Perez aimed his rifle at the Taliban soldier on the rooftop.

A soft thump sounded, and the man on the roof collapsed in place.

"One bogey down," Maurice murmured into his mic. "Might be more."

"Go," Perez said and covered Maurice as he moved forward.

"We have the target building in view," Scott said.

Maurice reached the end of a squat house and peered around the corner. A larger structure backed up to a hillside. Two men dressed in black leaned against the wall on either side of the door, holding rifles in their hands.

Perez slipped up behind Maurice.

Collins' voice sounded in Maurice's ear. "Tingle and I are in place, with the rear of the building in sight. It's built into the hill. No one's coming out the back unless they have tunnels exiting somewhere else. Heading your way to cover."

"Scott, take the guy on the right," Maurice said. "I got the left on three." Maurice raised his goggles, fitted his rifle against his shoulder and sighted in on the Taliban soldier. He spoke softly, "One...two..." As he said the word "three," he squeezed the trigger.

The two guards slumped and slid to the ground, their rifles clattering against the hard-packed dirt.

The team moved in.

Collins and Tingle positioned themselves on the corners of the building to provide cover on the outside while Maurice, Perez, Scott and Rusty entered.

Maurice took point.

They cleared one room at a time, finding boxes, crates and trash. No humans.

A door at the end of the hall opened into a tunnel that burrowed into the side of the hill.

Before stepping through the doorway, Maurice spoke into his mic. "Going into a tunnel. Will lose contact with Collins and Tingle."

"We've got your back," Collins said.

More worried that no one had their backs, Maurice said, "If shit gets real out there, join us inside. The building is clear. Our targets must be in the cave."

"Roger," Collins responded.

Wire ran the length of the tunnel, with an occasional yellow light bulb dangling along the way.

Thirty feet in, the tunnel curved sharply to the left.

Maurice slowed and held up his fist.

The men following him stopped, guns ready.

Maurice eased around the turn to find the tunnel opened into a small cavern lit by a few scattered light bulbs strung across the ceiling.

The stench of urine and unwashed bodies hit Maurice first. Men lay on mats across the floor. On the far side of the cavern, several cells had been carved out of the mountain. Metal bars had been fashioned into doors and hung over the cells. Something or someone moved inside one of the cells.

A low moan echoed softly through the cavern. A couple of the sleeping men stirred and went back to sleep. One man rose, walked to a corner to Maurice's left and peed in a bucket.

Maurice counted nine Taliban.

He backed around the corner and whispered to the men with him, "Small cavern. Nine bogeys, eight sleeping. Cells on the far side. Ready to roll?"

The other three nodded.

Again, on point, Maurice led the others into the cavern.

The man taking a piss was just finishing when Maurice slipped up behind him and dispatched him with his Ka-Bar knife. The man didn't even whimper as Maurice eased him to the floor.

Scott, Rusty and Perez took out a Taliban each before someone near Scott woke, sat up and shouted.

The remaining five Taliban leaped to their feet.

Two of the men were too late. Rusty and Perez

were on them before they could raise their weapons.

As the last three men started firing, Maurice flattened to a prone position and took out another man, careful not to aim in the direction of the cells.

Rusty and Perez dropped low and opened fire on the last two.

In less than two minutes, the room-cave was silent, the scent of gunpowder and blood mixing with the urine and body odor.

When he was certain none of the enemy remained alive, Maurice rose. "Let's go." He and Perez hurried toward the cells.

The cells were secured with padlocks.

"Find the key," Perez called out. "One of those bastards has to have it on him."

Scott and Rusty turned over dead men until they found the one with a keyring hanging from his belt.

Scott tossed the keyring to Maurice.

After three attempts, he found the one for the padlock he was working on and opened the gate. He handed the keyring to Perez, who worked the other gate.

Inside the cell, Maurice found a man stripped down to his boxers, his back covered in long, angry slashes, and his feet caked in dried blood. He didn't move when Maurice squatted beside him and felt for a pulse.

Maurice swore beneath his breath at the abuse the young man had suffered. But he had a pulse. If they could get him to help, he might live. He hefted the man onto his shoulder in a fireman's hold and carried him out of the cell into the cavern.

Perez had the other man, who was equally brutalized. A moan sounded from Perez's guy.

With Scott in the lead and Rusty following, they picked their way across the cavern and moved as quickly as possible through the tunnel.

Just as Scott reached out to push the door open into the building, Collins yanked it open, his face tense, his lips pressed into a tight line. "We gotta hustle. We've got company." He didn't wait for a response but turned and rushed back toward the front of the structure.

"Where's Tingle?" Maurice asked as he followed Collins, the weight of his charge slowing his steps.

"I'm on top of the building," Tingle said into Maurice's ear. "We've got a couple of truckloads of enemy heading our way. They're only about thirty yards away. They'll be within sight in thirty seconds or less. Get out. I'll cover."

"Come down now, and head for the exfil site," Maurice said.

They'd reached the front.

Collins burst through the door, rifle ready. Scott was out next.

Maurice followed. Then Perez.

Tingle, Collins and Scott covered while Maurice and Perez headed back the way they'd entered the village, with Rusty leading the way. The rest of the team fell in behind them, covering them from the rear.

Gunfire sounded behind Maurice as he entered a narrow alleyway. He didn't stop. Didn't slow. The team had his back. That's all he could hope. He and Perez had to get the injured soldiers to the extraction point before the truckloads of trouble caught up with them.

From the sounds behind him, the enemy was hot on their tail. Closing in fast.

Breathing hard, Maurice could hear Rusty radioing for the helicopter. Moments later, they reached the edge of the village.

The helicopter swept in and lowered over the exfil location. Ten feet off the ground, the chopper exploded in a fiery burst, sending rotor blades and shrapnel in all directions.

His heart in his throat, Maurice dropped to the

ground with his burden. Those people on the downed helicopter were gone. They'd been his friends.

A second Black Hawk appeared, the gunner hanging out the side, firing into an area fifty yards to the left of where the SEAL team hunkered down.

The gunner in the backup helicopter unloaded hell on the source of the RPG that had taken out the first aircraft.

Soon, the second chopper lowered to the ground near, but not too near, where the other had crashed.

"Move! Move! Move!" Collins yelled into Maurice's ear. "We're outnumbered ten to one, and they have RPGS."

Maurice rose, pulled his charge over his shoulder and ran toward the helicopter as it touched ground.

"Collin's hit!" Scott yelled into Maurice's headset.

"Can you get him to the chopper?" Maurice barked into his mic.

"Got him," Scott grunted. "Son of a bitch is heavy as fuck. But I got him."

"I'm almost there. Tingle and Rusty, cover and get your asses to the bird."

Maurice ducked as low as he could as he approached the Black Hawk's whirling rotors.

The gunner, hanging halfway out of the door, watched for the rest of the team.

Maurice lowered the soldier onto the floor of the helicopter and looked up into the face of the medic. His heart sank deep into his gut. Anger rose quickly to follow. "God damn it, Sandy. What the hell are you doing here? Jordan was supposed to cover this mission."

"He fell and broke his hand on his way to the chopper. Someone had to take his place. I was there. I came." She helped him drag the soldier deeper into the helicopter.

"Got another incoming," Maurice said and turned to help Perez load the injured soldier into the aircraft.

The gunner jerked the machine gun around and fired rounds over the heads of the rest of the team racing for the Black Hawk.

Once the soldier was in, Sandy moved to check for a pulse.

Maurice spun around and added his firepower to the gunner's, shooting over the heads of his teammates at the Taliban soldiers pouring out of the edge of the village.

Scott lumbered toward the chopper, carrying

Collins. Tingle and Rusty close behind, backs to the chopper, firing at the enemy.

Maurice met Scott halfway. Between the two men, they slid Collins onto the floor of the aircraft.

Sandy went to work on Collins, applying pressure to the wound on his thigh.

The gunner aimed the full force of the M240A machine gun at the enemy while Maurice and Scott helped Tingle and Rusty aboard and jumped in after.

Maurice was barely inside when the Black Hawk rose from the ground, rocking with a sudden wind shear.

Sandy knelt beside Collins in the doorway, ripped open the medical bag and pulled out a saline IV bag. "Hold this!" she yelled over the roar of the engine, rotors and the blasts of the machine gun.

Maurice moved past her to give her room, hooked his hand in a cargo strap to stabilize, then grabbed the saline bag and held it while Sandy eased a needle into Collins's arm with quiet, determined efficiency. Calm, focused and good at what she did. That was Sandy. She didn't unravel in the heat of battle.

God, he loved her.

"Incoming!" the gunner yelled.

A flash erupted outside the open door, shooting sparks like a magnesium fire. The force of the explosion rocked the helicopter, immediately followed by a thick white cloud rushing into the craft along with the sound of something, not shrapnel, pelting the metal sides of the fuselage.

The scent of garlic, chemicals and burning hair assailed Maurice's nostrils.

Sandy jerked, her back arching violently. She screamed as a flash of fire rose from the back of her helmet.

The Black Hawk lurched sideways.

Sandy's knees slid in blood. She tipped backward, arms flailing, toward the open door.

Maurice released the cargo strap, dropped the IV bag and lunged for Sandy, grabbing her by the front of her armor-plated vest. Her momentum pulled him after her. They teetered at the edge of the door, rotor wash sucking at them. The helicopter rose higher into the air, several hundred feet from the ground.

Someone grabbed Maurice from behind.

Needing a better grasp on Sandy, Maurice released his right hand on the front of her vest and reached for a better hold, his fist bunching in the back of her body armor. Something sizzled against his fingers. The pain burned through his hand. He roared in anger. He couldn't let go—wouldn't let go of Sandy.

Then, hands on his arms and legs dragged him back from the door.

He brought Sandy with him.

Not until she was out of danger of falling from the craft did he release her vest and stare down at his hand, melting before his eyes.

"White phosphorous!" Scott yelled. He snagged the IV bag from the floor, punched a hole in it with his knife, held it over Maurice's hand and squirted it over the flesh-eating chemical. The smell of burning flesh filled his senses.

He pushed Scott aside and dropped to his knees beside Sandy.

She lay face down, her body spasming, her fingers clawing at the metal floor.

"Careful!" Scott yelled. "The phosphorus got on her."

Tingle held a flashlight over Sandy, the beam revealing a dark burn spot on the back of her helmet.

Maurice reached beneath her chin and unbuckled the clip. Holding onto the strap, he eased the helmet from her head and flung it out the door.

Tingle swept the flashlight beam over the back of Sandy's head and muttered, "Fuck."

A dark spot at the base of her skull told the story. She'd been hit by white phosphorous.

"Give me water! Gauze! Saline! Anything!" Maurice cried. He pulled Sandy up into his arms while others dug into the medic bag. "Sandy. Hold on. We've got you. Hang in there, baby."

Her eyes stared up at him, unfocused, her body limp in his arms.

Scott dropped down beside Maurice. "Lean her forward."

Maurice tipped her over his arm. Her head drooped, exposing the back of her neck where flesh and hair had been burned away.

Scott poured saline over a wad of gauze and dabbed at the spot.

"Just pour it on, damn it," Maurice barked.

Scott squeezed the bag over the spot until it was empty.

Maurice leaned Sandy back. Her head lolled to the side. "Sandy?" He laid her out next to Collins and touched the fingers of his left hand to the base of her throat, praying for a pulse.

"Sandy, baby, don't quit on me now. We have plans. A December wedding. Honeymoon in Cabo. Stay with me."

Scott pushed his hand aside and touched his fingers to her throat. For a long moment, he waited. He dug in the medic bag again, found a pen light and lifted one of Sandy's eyelids. The pupils didn't respond. He tried the other with the same result.

Beside them, Rusty tied a tourniquet around Collins's leg and applied a pressure bandage to his wound.

And Sandy lay still, her face pale, body limp.

A hand touched his shoulder. He didn't look up. Words were useless. No tourniquet or pressure bandage would save her. Nothing Maurice could do would bring her back.

CHAPTER 1

"You can't leave now," Felina Faivre cried. "They're playing the Cupid Shuffle." She grabbed Amelie Aubert's arm and dragged her toward the dance floor, where their group of friends lined up, laughing and swaying to the intro.

"I've been up since three-thirty," Amelie said, digging in her heels. "If I leave now, I might get five hours of sleep before I have to get up at three-thirty again."

"Just one more dance," Felina begged with a hint of a whine.

At the pleading look from the green eyes of Bayou Mambaloa's favorite florist, Amelie gave in. However, she stopped at the edge of the dance floor to give herself clearance to make her escape after the current song finished.

"This is the first time in months we've had most of us at a girl's night out." Felina moved her feet in time to the music and the others performing the line dance. "We have to make the most of it before more of us drop babies."

Amelie's eyebrows rose. "Are you trying to tell me you're pregnant?"

"Felina's pregnant?" Holly Gautier paused on her way to deliver a tray of drinks to a table full of rowdy men. She spoke loudly enough that the other girls in their group heard and gathered around Felina.

Camille, their local candymaker, grabbed Felina's arm. "You're pregnant?"

"No. No." Felina's cheeks pinkened.

"Felina's pregnant?" Shelby Taylor engulfed Felina in a big hug. "That's awesome. Your baby can join Bernie's Gabby and my sweet Jean-Luc at our play dates."

Gisele, the granddaughter of Bayou Mambaloa's Voodoo queen, demanded, "Why wasn't I told?"

"Because I'm not." Felina extricated herself from Shelby's hug and grimaced. "Yet." She looked at her friends. "Lucas and I are trying. We've met with a fertility specialist."

"Oh, sweetie," Bernie took Felina's hand. "It will happen."

"And if it doesn't?" Felina's eyes glazed.

"There are lots of children who need loving parents," Ouida Mae said. "Like my Sophie and Harley Quinn." She'd adopted Sophie as a pregnant fourteen-year-old and then adopted the baby she'd given birth to months later.

"And my Billy Ray is a great big brother to Ava." Camille smiled. "She thinks he hung the moon."

Felina sighed. "We haven't ruled out adoption. But we wanted to try to have one of our own first. In truth, the trying is the most fun." She grinned and waved toward the dance floor. "Come on, ladies. We should be dancing."

As their friends surrounded Felina in solidarity, Amelie stayed at the edge of the dance floor, feeling more disconnected than ever. Most of her friends had husbands or lovers now, leaving her the odd girl out. The third wheel. Their single friend. If they weren't all so busy with their own perfect lives, they'd probably try to set her up on blind dates.

Amelie shook her head. She'd been in Bayou Mambaloa for a few years now. She'd made friends and then watched as they'd fallen in love with the men of the Bayou Brotherhood Protectors.

Because she was the town baker, Amelie's hours made dating difficult. Plus, she wasn't sure she was ready to date.

She'd come to Bayou Mambaloa to escape. To make a new life for herself. A different life than she'd imagined as a young twenty-one-year-old who'd moved to Paris to train and build a career as a chef.

As she moved through the line dance, she remembered.

Her first day in Paris. Alone. Following a dream to become a chef. She'd spent nine months at Le Cordon Bleu Culinary School, then interning at *Maison Belle Époque* for a year. When she'd received a personal invitation to intern at *Chez Benoît*, Amelie had been beside herself. Only the best culinary students in Paris received invitations to study under the world-renowned Chef Armand Benoît. He'd come from a long line of highly respected French chefs, continuing a legacy of unequaled perfection in the culinary world.

Armand had been tough but fair. If he didn't see passion in his students, he didn't waste his time on them.

After a few weeks, he'd taken Amelie under his wing, treating her more like one of his children than his own son. He'd taught her the magic of culinary art—the beauty of exquisite cuisine.

She'd transitioned from student to sous chef. The bond between Amelie and Armand had grown over the years. He hadn't been just the head chef and instructor, he'd been a friend. A father-figure. Someone she'd trusted and who trusted her.

Four years under Armand's tutelage hadn't been nearly enough, yet it had been all she would have.

Near the end of her fourth anniversary working with Amand, he'd gifted her with his family's prized recipe book that had been passed down through the ages. She'd tried to refuse the book, stating it should go to his son, Luis, to keep it in the family.

Armand had insisted she keep it safe, the secrets within for her eyes only. Luis wouldn't know what to do with it. After multiple attempts with chef oversight, he had yet to make a palatable *Soufflé au Fromage.* Though he loved his son, he doubted the young man would carry on the Benoît legacy. Armand wanted *le grand livre de la cuisine* to go to someone who would treasure its importance and keep it safe and secret from everyone, including Luis.

To Amelie, the book had been the ultimate gift,

a profound honor. She'd spent that evening and well into the night carefully leafing through the pages, her excitement and wonder making it impossible to sleep. She'd loved the handwritten notes in the margines, knowing the hands that had made them belonged to people Armand had loved.

The next morning, she'd hurried to the restaurant to thank Armand again for the gift, only to find her mentor dead on the floor of his kitchen. Authorities ruled he'd had a heart attack.

"You must really dislike the Cupid Shuffle," a voice said over the music.

Amelie pulled her thoughts back to the present and turned to face Maurice Boucher, one of the members of the Bayou Brotherhood Protectors who had moved to Bayou Mambaloa almost two years before. He stood still on the edge of the dance floor.

Amelie missed a turn, caught up and fell in line again. "Why do you think I don't like the dance?"

Maurice gave her a crooked smile. "You've been frowning through most of the song. I could buy you a drink to save you from line-dance hell, if you think it would help."

His offer tempted her. Performing the line dance while reminiscing over that fateful day when she'd lost her friend wasn't a good combination.

"I was lost in thought." She shook her head. "I promised the ladies I'd do this last dance before I left." Amelie tipped her head toward the line. "You could join us."

"I could if I didn't have two left feet."

"This is perhaps the easiest line dance on record." She missed another step and muttered, "Not that I'm a good example."

"Tell you what," Maurice said. "I'll try if you promise me the next slow dance. It's more my speed."

"I really have to go. You know," she shrugged, "life of a baker and all. Donuts don't cook themselves early in the morning."

"I get it, and I wouldn't want you to disappoint your customers, me being one of them." He stepped up beside her, watched her feet move and joined in, catching on quickly.

"Two left feet, huh?" Amelie rolled her eyes.

"It appears you were right. This line dance, I can do."

After another repetition, the song ended.

Amelie's girl squad hurried toward their table, leaving her standing with Maurice as the DJ played the next song. Her lips twisted when she realized it was a slow dance.

Maurice held out his hands. "You wouldn't leave a man standing alone on the dance floor, would you?"

Amelie looked around the room at all the single women eyeing the man like a juicy side of beef. "There are enough single women, ready to pounce; you wouldn't be alone for long."

"Then save me from being pounced upon." Maurice took one of her hands and gently pulled her into his arms.

Something about his right hand felt off. She glanced at where it held hers and frowned. "Why is it I've never noticed that you're missing part of your finger?"

He shrugged. "Because you've been so busy with your bakery and keeping Bayou Mambaloa hopped-up on sugar to notice much else." His brow dipped. "If it bothers you, we don't have to hold hands to slow dance."

"No," she tightened her hold. "It's fine."

"The hand is the least you have to worry about. If I step on your feet, you have my permission to stomp on mine. Or you can walk away at any time."

"Oh, shut up and dance," she said and leaned

into his body, liking that she could rest her cheek against his neck and smell the woodsy scent of his cologne.

She swayed to the music, her gaze going to the ladies who'd missed the opportunity to pounce on the tall, handsome man.

His good hand rested against the middle of her back, while the other held hers, strong yet gentle.

Was this what it had been like for her friends who'd found their guys? She'd thought she was envious before. Now, she was downright jealous.

How long had it been since she'd been held in a man's arms? He made her feel all warm and tingly.

"So, was the line dance what was making you frown? Or was it something else?" he whispered against her ear.

And like that, the warmth and tingles disappeared, and she stiffened.

Maurice leaned back and stared down into her eyes. "Sorry. I take it you were having some unpleasant thoughts. Do I need to punch someone in the face for you?"

She smiled. "No. That won't be necessary. I wasn't mad at anyone. Just remembering."

"Still stands," Maurice said. "Do I need to punch someone in the face?"

"I was remembering the loss of a very dear man," she said.

"I'm sorry," he said softly, holding her closer. "It's hard to lose someone you love."

She nodded, sinking back into the memories.

At Armand's funeral, she'd stood beside his son, Luis, mourning the loss of a father, mentor and friend. The emotion had cut so deep it had hurt physically.

Her world, her trajectory, everything had changed from that moment. Her mentor. Gone. Her career as a sous chef in France. Over. The restaurant closed and was sold.

Heartbroken at the loss of Armand, Amelie couldn't stay in the city that reminded her of the man who'd taught her so much about the kitchen, life and a different kind of passion.

She'd left Paris and returned to Louisiana, where she'd searched for work in New Orleans, thinking it was as close to her home in the bayou as she could get and still practice her skills as a chef.

With her resume, she was hired within a couple of weeks, landing a job as sous chef at one of the most exclusive French restaurants.

Learning the ways of her chef and the restaurant had kept her busy, kept her moving through her grief. But working and living in New Orleans hadn't filled the hole in her heart. Amelie had trudged through her days, wanting more, needing connection, but hadn't found it in the city.

When her apartment had been vandalized while she'd been working one evening, she'd been shocked and frightened. What if she'd been in the apartment when the criminals had broken down her door and torn through her belongings? The destruction added to Amelie's grief and longing for a safe haven.

"Hey," Maurice spoke softly. "Are you all right?"

Amelie blinked up at him, coming back to the present—to the arms wrapped around her and the silence following what must have been the end of the song and the set.

"The band is taking a break." Maurice's arms lowered. He took her hand. "Let me buy you a drink. I think you need one. You were back in that dark place."

She grimaced. "I try hard not to get lost in my memories. They sneak in on me when I'm tired."

"You should go home and get some rest," Maurice said.

"That's my plan," Amelie said. "Thank you for the dance. I'm sorry I wasn't very lively."

"I wasn't looking for lively," Maurice said.

Amelie tilted her head as she met his gaze. "What *were* you looking for?"

He gave her a twisted smile. "I wasn't actually looking for anything. But when I saw you at the edge of the dance floor, I felt like I'd found what I was looking for." Maurice shrugged. "Sounds weird when I say it like that. I guess I felt like you needed to be rescued from your own thoughts."

"And you rescued me." She squeezed the hand holding hers. "At least you helped me by reminding me I wasn't alone. Thank you. Now," she glanced toward the table where her girl squad had gone, "I'll say goodnight to my friends and go get that rest I'm sure I need."

Instead of dropping her hand, Maurice held onto it and walked her back to where Gisele, Bernie, Felina, Camille and Shelby laughed as their friend and waitress, Holly, unloaded a round of drinks onto their table.

As Amelie approached, they all looked up, their gazes zeroing in on her hand in Maurice's.

Shelby was first to comment. "Ah, Maurice, so glad you managed to keep Amelie out on the floor for another song. She works entirely too hard and deserves a break."

Maurice grinned. "It was entirely my pleasure."

Amelie smiled at him and pulled her hand free.

"No, it was mine." She faced her friends. "I have to leave now, or I won't be functional at three in the morning to make fresh donuts, beignets and cinnamon rolls."

"Oh, and don't forget the petit fours," Camille said. "My favorites are the pistachios."

"Ladies, goodnight," Amelie said. "It's been fun. Let's not wait so long to do it again."

"Agreed." Camille rose from her seat and wrapped her arms around Amelie. "We love you so much."

"And we love your baking even more," Gisele said with a wink.

Shelby, ever the sheriff's deputy even when off duty, rose. "I'll follow you home."

Amelie shook her head. "That won't be necessary. "I'm perfectly capable of driving myself home. You all stay and enjoy."

"Perhaps Maurice can escort you home." Camille cocked an eyebrow and smiled in Maurice's direction.

"I'd be happy to," Maurice said.

Already shaking her head, Amelie touched his arm. "Really, I don't need an escort." She nodded toward the table full of Brotherhood Protectors. "I'm sure you'd rather stay and visit with your friends."

Maurice shook his head. "I'm ready to call it a night." He raised a hand toward his friends. "The way they look, they're in it for the long haul. Besides, I see them all the time." He smiled at Amelie. "So, it's settled. I'll follow you home to make sure you get there safely."

Not wanting to make a scene or appear ungrateful, Amelie nodded. "Okay, then. I'm ready when you are."

As her friends waved goodbye, Amelie left the Crawdad Hole Bar and Grill with Maurice.

In the parking lot, she approached the little car she'd purchased second-hand when she'd returned from France. It wasn't fancy and didn't have all the bells and whistles, but it got her around.

After Amelie unlocked the door, Maurice reached around her to open it for her.

"Thanks," she said and slipped into the driver's seat.

"I'll be behind you in my truck." Maurice closed the door.

Amelie watched as he walked away. He had really broad shoulders and narrow hips—and he could dance. A triple threat, in her books. Though she envied her friends' love lives, she didn't envy them enough to do anything about her own. She'd been too busy building her business in Bayou Mambaloa to care about dating.

Still...

It had been nice to lean into him when her memories and grief had weighed heavily in her heart. He'd made her feel less alone.

Maybe she'd be ready to spend time in the company of a man soon. A man who recognized a troubled soul on the edge of a dance floor, going through the moves when her heart wasn't in it. A man like Maurice.

Amelie squared her shoulders and started the car.

The engine ground lethargically and died.

She tried to start it again, but with the same result.

On her third attempt, the engine didn't even rumble. The car was dead.

She glanced through the windshield to find Maurice headed back toward her and her vehicle.

Her cheeks heated. It appeared she'd get to spend more time with him sooner rather than later. Had her wishful thinking manifested the stranded vehicle?

As he neared, she pushed her door open. "Won't start."

"Pop the hood," he said, and walked around to the front of the vehicle.

Amelie pulled the lever that unlocked the latch.

Maurice lifted the hood and disappeared beneath it.

"Try again," he called out.

She did.

And...

Nothing.

Only a clicking sound. Not engine rumbles or signs of life.

"Could be a dead battery or the starter." He closed the hood. "Or both. Do you want me to call for a wrecker?"

Amelie grabbed her purse and got out of the vehicle. "I'll do it in the morning. If I need to get around, I can use the bakery's delivery van."

"In the meantime, can I offer you a ride home?" Maurice asked.

Amelie glanced toward the building. She didn't want to interrupt her friends enjoying their girls' night out. She turned a tired smile on Maurice. "Yes, please."

He held out his arm.

Amelie hooked her hand into the crook of his elbow and let him lead her to the passenger side of his pickup.

He opened the door and handed her up into his vehicle. In the next moment, he stepped up onto the running board, leaned over her and buckled her seatbelt in place.

Amelie's heart fluttered as she inhaled his woodsy cologne. "I—" she squeaked, cleared her throat and continued, "could have done that myself."

He dropped to the ground and grinned up at her. "But where's the fun in that?" His lips twisted. "That buckle can be a little finicky. I thought I'd spare you the frustration."

She snorted, but bit down on her lip to keep from telling him that he'd caused more frustration than he'd spared.

How long had it been since she'd been with a man?

Apparently, too long.

"Thank you," she murmured instead.

Maurice closed her door, rounded the front of the truck and slid into the driver's seat. Resting his arm across the back of her seat, he looked over his shoulder and backed out of the parking space. Once he'd driven out onto the highway, he shot her a glance. "By the way, I should be thanking you."

She frowned. "For what?"

"For giving me an excuse to leave early. I wasn't feeling it tonight."

"Why?" she asked.

He shrugged. "I get this way when I'm in between assignments."

"I thought the boat factory kept your team busy when you're not on assignment."

"Usually, it does. But the boat production is in between projects as well. We're waiting on supplies."

"How do you like making boats?" she asked. "It's a lot different than being a bodyguard."

He smiled. "I like the hands-on aspect and getting to see the end result. Most of the security services we provide are pretty much hands-off. There's something to be said for seeing the fruits of your labor. It's gratifying."

Amelie nodded. "I get that. In my case, I get to see, touch and taste what I make with my hands."

"And then it's consumed, with gratification expressed by your customers."

"Happy customers are the goal."

"Same with the boats, only they last longer than a really great pastry."

"True," Amelie admitted. "But the memory of that exceptional pastry keeps them coming back for more."

"Speaking of exceptional dishes," he said, "have you always been a baker?"

Amelie shook her head. "No. Baking was only part of my previous work. But when I came home to Bayou Mambaloa, I didn't think a town this small would warrant a five-star French restaurant, nor did I have the funds to build or staff one." She shrugged. "Running a bakery made more sense. It didn't require a big building, and I could run it myself, although I think I've got enough business now to hire a helper soon."

"You always have customers going in and out of your place. I'm surprised you do it all on your own. What do you do when you want to take a day off?"

"I close the shop on Mondays. That gives me time to go into New Orleans if I need supplies I can't have delivered or if I want to get my hair or nails done." She looked down at her nails. "Not that I've done either of those things lately."

"Where did you learn to cook?" Maurice asked as he drove slowly down Main Street.

"From my mother, at first." Amelie frowned because the memories flooded back. "Then in Paris."

"And you're frowning again," Maurice said softly. "Is that where you lost him?"

Amelie nodded. Thankfully, Maurice pulled up

to her bakery, ending the conversation. She gave Maurice a weak smile. "Thank you for giving me a ride home. I'll call the wrecker service in the morning to have them pick up my car." She pushed open her door and dropped to the ground.

As she reached the front of the truck, Maurice appeared in front of her.

"You don't have to walk me to the door," she said.

He held up his hand. "I know. You're a strong, independent woman, capable of walking to your apartment on your own. However, my mother taught me that a man isn't a gentleman if he doesn't walk a woman to her door. That, and it's in my nature and the job description to ensure the safety of the people around me." He held out his arm. "That would be you." When she didn't take his arm, he added. "Please. Just humor me. If not for yourself, then for my mother."

Her lips twitched as she slipped her hand into the crook of his elbow. "For your mother."

"Thank you." He tipped his head toward the sky. "Did you hear that, Mom? Your lessons didn't fall on deaf ears."

Amelie stopped in front of the bakery, her brow dipping. "When did you lose your mother?"

He stared at the door, his face reflecting his sadness in the glass. "I was on a mission in Afghanistan when I got word she was sick with the flu. By the time I got to where I could call to check on her, she'd passed."

Her hand tightened on his arm. "You didn't get to say goodbye."

He shook his head. "No, and they'd already had the funeral, not knowing when I'd be out of the field."

"It's hard to get closure."

"Yeah. It didn't seem real to me. I didn't see her get sick and watch her body shut down. I didn't see her at the funeral. I was in denial for the longest, thinking she'd show up and tease me that I could be fooled so easily."

"But she didn't." Amelie sighed.

"No. She didn't." He looked down at her hand on his arm. "At least with my father, I was there with him when he passed ten months later." His lips pressed into a tight line. "The doctors said his heart gave out. They called it broken heart syndrome." He lifted his head. "Wow. I shouldn't have weighed you down with more depressing thoughts. You were already down, thinking about someone you'd loved and lost." He covered her hand with his. "You need to get inside, switch on a sitcom and cleanse your mind of death and dying." He looked at the door. "You live above the bakery, don't you?"

She nodded. "Yes. The stairs to my apartment are around the back."

Maurice frowned as he walked her around the side of the building. "You need more light and security cameras."

Amelie was thinking the same thing. "There's usually more light than this, and it has a motion-sensor device." She glanced up at the fixture on the corner that wasn't doing its job. "Is it my imagination, or is that light broken?"

Maurice tipped his head and studied the corner light. "It's broken." Quietly, he removed her hand from his arm, shifted to place his body in front of hers and leaned his head around the corner. "Did you leave the back door to your shop open?"

"No," she said and started around him, her heart in her throat.

Maurice raised his arm, blocking her path. "Stay here," he whispered. "If someone broke in, he might still be there."

"Then we should call the sheriff," she said.

"You do that…from here," he said. "I'm going in to check it out." He took a step away.

"Or," Amelie grabbed his hand, "you can stay here with me and wait for the police to come."

"If he's in there, I don't want him to get away."

"And I don't want you to get hurt," she squeezed his hand harder. "What if he's armed?"

"Then I disarm him and hold him until the police come." He lifted her hand to his lips. "Don't worry. I won't do anything stupid. I just want to see if he's still there. I won't go in if I hear anyone moving around. Deal?"

She frowned. "You're going to go in no matter what I say, aren't you?"

He nodded. "And you're going to call the sheriff."

She took her cell phone out of her purse. "Calling now."

"Going now." He pulled his hand from hers.

Amelie dialed 911 as Maurice eased toward the back door of the bakery and cocked his head. Listening.

Amelie tiptoed after him, more afraid of standing alone in the dark than entering her bakery where an intruder might be lurking.

Maurice glanced over his shoulder, noted that she stood not three yards from him and nodded his approval. He must not have liked leaving her alone either. He held up his hand, indicating she should stop short of the door.

The dispatcher answered Amelie's call as Maurice ducked into the bakery.

CHAPTER 2

MAURICE HADN'T HEARD anything from inside the bakery. He might really have waited for the police, since he was pretty sure the intruder was gone. The white powder strewn across the floor was the best indicator. Footprints through the powder lead out the back.

To make sure the place was empty, he flipped on the light switch and went in. He was careful not to disturb the footprints in case the sheriff could match them to a specific shoe, though it seemed unlikely, as much of the fine dust had been smeared.

The bakery was a mess with the fine white dust covering nearly every surface. The consistency of the powder made Maurice believe it was flour. He found a large sack ripped down the middle as if someone had stabbed it with a knife. The source of the flour. Cannisters of other ingredients had been emptied, recipe books and books containing pictures of wedding and birthday cakes had been slung across the floor. Refrigerators and ovens stood open and every cabinet door hung ajar.

Nothing moved. No one hid in the storage closet or behind the display counter. Whoever had been there had done the damage and left.

Maurice hurried back out to find Amelie standing next to the back door, speaking softly to the dispatcher. She met his gaze.

"It's empty."

"Did you hear that, Minnie?" she asked. "Okay. We'll wait for Stewie. Thanks." She ended the call and glanced through the door. "How bad is it?"

"It's a mess," he said. "Did you have any valuables in the register or a safe?"

Amelie shook her head. "I take my deposits to the bank every evening and only keep enough money in the register to make change. So many people prefer to use credit cards these days. Was there any equipment damaged?" she asked, craning her neck to see inside. "Is that flour all over the floor?"

"I assume it's flour, as the sack it was in has a giant hole in it. I couldn't see any damage to equipment, but every door was open, including the refrigerators and ovens."

"We need to close the refrigerator doors, so what's inside won't spoil." She started to go inside and stopped. "No. It doesn't matter. There's no telling what the vandal touched or disturbed. I'll have to toss everything and start over with supplies." She wrapped her arms around her middle and shook her head. "Who would do this?"

"I don't know." He glanced at the corners of the building and the light over the back porch. "Do you have security cameras?"

She sighed. "Not yet. I ordered a system a week ago. It should be here tomorrow." Her lips pulled downward on the corners. "I was going to install it next Monday."

"And you still will. I'll help." Maurice's gaze followed the white powdery prints that led off the porch, fading with each step the perp had taken. They led away from the back door and toward...

"Is that the staircase to your apartment?" he asked, already knowing the answer.

"It is." Amelie's frown deepened. "Do you think he went up there?"

Maurice stared at the bottom step where a trace of flour answered her question.

Before Maurice could stop her, Amelie raced up the steps and pushed through the open door.

Maurice took the steps two at a time, arriving at the top to find the doorframe splintered, the door hanging slightly open and Amelie standing in the small apartment, staring around at the destruction.

Maurice flipped the light switch and hurried toward the woman. He pulled her against him, shielding her body with his as he looked around, braced for attack.

Silence surrounded them.

He nodded toward the only other door leading off the combination living room and kitchen. "That your bedroom?"

"Yes," she said.

He pinned her gaze with his. "Will you stay here while I check it out?"

She nodded and sniffed. "Yes."

He ducked into her bedroom, checked beneath the bed, in the closet and the bathroom, stepping around or over drawers that had been pulled from the dresser, clothes that had been ripped from the closet and the mattress that hung halfway off the bed.

He returned to the living room where Amelie

stood as if shell-shocked, her face pale, her arms wrapped around herself.

The wail of a siren sounded in the distance.

Maurice pulled her into his arms. "It's just stuff," he said.

She rested her cheek against his chest. "I know. But it's terrifying that someone could get in so easily and destroy so much." She shook her head. "I've only been gone a couple of hours. What if I'd been home when he'd busted in?"

"You weren't here. He probably knew it."

Her fingers curled into his shirt. "Oh, God. He could've been watching me. That's even creepier."

"The important thing to focus on is that you're okay. You're safe."

She leaned back and stared up into his eyes, frowning. "I won't be able to open the shop tomorrow. I don't know how long it'll take to clean up this mess, and I'll need all new supplies."

"When the sheriff gets here, you'll need to look through everything and see if you're missing anything."

She glanced around her apartment. "I don't own anything of much value except for the ovens and refrigerators. It's not like he could abscond with them that easily."

When a sheriff's vehicle pulled up outside the

bakery, Maurice and Amelie descended the stairs and met him out front.

Stewie took pictures, dusted for latent prints and took Amelie and Maurice's statements. "I'm sorry this happened to you, Amelie. You know how much we all love your bakery. We'll do our best to find out who did it."

Stewie was just wrapping up when Deputy Shelby Taylor arrived in her personal vehicle.

As soon as she parked, she jumped out and ran to Amelie. "Oh, sweetie, we were just leaving the Crawdad Hole when I heard, or I would've been here sooner." She hugged her friend. "You should've called me."

Amelie grimaced. "I called 911. You're not even on duty. You should be on your way home to your baby, not here."

"I'm always there for my friends. Besides, Remy relieved the babysitter. Jean-Luc is in good hands." Shelby tipped her head toward Maurice. "I'm glad you didn't come home alone like you wanted. I'm sure it would've been even more of a shock. And dangerous. What if the vandal had still been here?" She shook her head. "I don't like it."

"Whoever did it was gone by the time we arrived," Amelie said. "But I'm glad Maurice was with me. I..." she shook her head, "it was like a punch in the gut."

"I'll bet it was." Shelby stared around the interior of the bakery. "Remy and I can come over in the morning to help clean up. I'm sure you've already given your statement, but was anything missing?"

"Not that I could tell," Amelie said.

Shelby frowned. "By the way, all the drawers are pulled out and the doors to the cabinets are open. Could he have been looking for something?"

Maurice frowned. "I had the same thought."

"I really don't own anything of value," Amelie said. "I don't wear expensive jewelry, mostly because I don't own any. I don't keep wads of cash lying around. I make daily deposits to avoid that. The cash register wasn't even opened. All the bills and change appeared untouched. If stealing something had been the goal, they would've taken the money."

"Any missing paintings, coin collections, electronics?" Shelby asked.

Amelie shook her head. "None of that. I put every bit of profit back into the business or in the bank."

"Maybe it was a group of teens looking for trouble," Shelby offered.

Maurice shook his head. "Teenaged boys would've eaten their way through the donuts and cookies."

"None of the displays were touched," Amelie said. "Just the drawers below. They were pulled out and dumped on the floor."

"Stewie, are you finished here?" Shelby asked the other deputy.

"Yes, ma'am," the tall, lanky man replied. "I'm heading out. "Are you going to be all right, Ms. Aubert? Do you need a place to stay tonight?"

Amelie pushed a hand through her hair. "I'm all right."

"She'll be staying with me," Shelby announced.

"No." Amelie held up a hand. "I'll stay in my own place. Besides, I need to dive in, clean, organize, make a plan and a grocery list. I can't afford to be closed for too long."

Shelby crossed her arms over her chest. "You can't stay here alone."

"It's not like I'll sleep," Amelie said. "I'll be awake, alert and ready to take anyone down who tries anything funny."

Shelby snorted. "And if he comes back, what are you going to do? Hit him with a fist-sized wad of pastry dough?"

Amelie's lips quirked. "Maybe."

"You can't stay here alone," Shelby persisted.

"I'll be with her," Maurice said.

Amelie frowned. "I don't need—"

Maurice touched one of his big fingers to her lips, liking how soft they were. "The right response is *thank you.* "No" is not an option."

Amelie met his gaze. "Okay, I know when I'm arguing with a stone wall." Her lips twisted into a wry grin. "To tell the truth, it would be nice to have someone who has my back. Fair warning, though... I'll be working all night."

"Can't you let it be for the night?" Shelby asked.

"No," Amelie said. "Right now, I'm too upset to consider sleep. Working and keeping busy is what I need. Making food, even desserts, is my therapy. The sooner I can clean up the evidence of destruction and get back to what I do best, the better."

Shelby focused on Maurice. "You'll stay all night?"

He nodded. "We'll be okay. I have a pistol in my truck. I'll bring it in for protection."

"I'd still rather Amelie came home with me," Shelby murmured.

Amelie touched her friend's arm. "Thanks for caring."

"I don't like it," Shelby said. "If you need anything, call 911 and then me.

"Got it," Amelie said. "Now, go home to your baby."

Shelby smiled. "He's such an angel when he's asleep." Her smile twisted. "Then he wakes up and keeps me on my toes all day long. I go to work now to get rest."

Amelie laughed. "And you wouldn't trade him for the world."

"No," Shelby said. "I love that little guy. And I love Remy. I don't know how I ever lived without them." She glanced at her watch. "I'll check in with you tomorrow. You'll be safe with Maurice. He's one of the good guys."

Shelby's departure left Amelie standing alone with Maurice. "You really don't have to stay. I can manage the cleanup on my own."

"It's already settled. I'm staying," he said. "Where do you want to start? In the shop or your apartment?"

"The shop," she said with a crisp, definitive nod. "I want to start by taking photos of everything for the insurance claim. Then I need to set things to rights, clean and make a list of the supplies I'll need to be back up and running as soon as possible. And I'll want to check all the equipment to make sure nothing was tampered with."

"I'm yours to command."

Amelie snapped photos of the damage done to the bakery, using her cell phone to capture multiple angles of the damages until she was satisfied. Maurice followed her up to the apartment, where she did the same.

As she finished in one room, he straightened furniture, put drawers back into cabinets and dressers and aligned the mattress with the bed.

Once Amelie had all the pictures she deemed necessary, they returned to the bakery below and started cleaning.

Maurice went straight to the worst offender— the ripped back of flour still spilling its contents from the hole in its middle. "Do you have a plastic trash bag we can deposit this into?"

She appeared behind him, holding a heavy-duty garbage bag open for him. She smiled at him. "Will this do?"

He nodded and gathered the torn bag from the shelf. As he turned, his foot slipped in the powdery flour on the floor. He pitched forward, aiming the leaking bag of flour toward the open garbage bag and praying it would find its mark.

When the sack made it into the trash bag, it landed with enough force to send a huge puff of flour into the air, depositing a thick coat of white powder on anything within a two-foot radius, including Amelie's hair, face and the arms holding the bag.

She blinked. White dust floated down, turning her black hair gray and coating her cheeks. She bent over, her shoulders shaking.

"Amelie, I'm so sorry." Maurice touched a hand to her back, noting how her body shook. "Are you okay?"

She pressed a hand to her side.

"Seriously, are you okay?" Maurice hovered over her.

She nodded without looking up. Then she dug her hand into the trash bag and raised it with a fist full of flour, her eyes sparkling with mischief in her powdered face.

Maurice held his hands up. "You wouldn't..."

"Watch me." She uncurled her fingers and blew flour into Maurice's face.

He staggered backward, blinking the dust from his eyes.

Amelie burst out laughing so hard she fell to her knees and sat in the flour blanketing the floor. She laughed until tears filled her eyes.

Stunned by Amelie's streak of playfulness, Maurice stood for a moment in shock, but then laughter bubbled up in his chest, and he joined her.

Slowly, Amelie's laughter choked off, the tears

spilling down her face left naked trails through the powder on her cheeks.

Maurice's laughter faded as he realized her burst of levity was a desperate release of adrenaline and shock.

He dropped down beside her and pulled her into his arms. For several minutes, they sat in silence amidst the mess of her bakery, her business, her livelihood.

He didn't offer any more words of encouragement. What could he say that he hadn't already? The best he could do was be there for her. She didn't have to face the destruction of her home and business alone.

He found that he liked holding her, feeling the warmth of her body pressed to his. Just when that thought occurred to him, she leaned back, squared her shoulders and said, "I really don't have time for a pity party."

"You're allowed a little time for it."

She shook her head. "Not when I have so much work to do." Her back stiffened along with her resolve.

Maurice stood, helped Amelie to her feet and held onto her hands a little longer than necessary, reluctant to release her.

"Thanks for letting me have a moment of

weakness." She gave him a watery smile. "I promise not to do it again."

"And the flour in the face?"

"Oh, I'd do that again," she said with a wink, and marched toward the storage room. A moment later, she returned with several large garbage bags. "We'll start by removing all the baked goods from the display cases and refrigerators."

"Seems like such a shame. The cakes and cookies look amazing."

"Maybe so, but I can't be sure the vandal didn't touch or poison them, God forbid."

Maurice sighed, his mouth watering as he scooped up trays of cupcakes, donuts and cookies and dumped them into the bag. "This is not only a crime of vandalism, but it's also a crime of the heart and stomach."

Amelie laughed. "Don't worry. I'll bake new goodies."

"When? I'm hungry now," he said and winked.

Her brow furrowed. "It won't be until I can purchase new supplies." She shook her head. "If I didn't know better, I'd think someone sabotaged my business to keep me from selling my goods."

Maurice paused with a tray of pastel-colored petit fours. "Is there another baker in Bayou

Mambaloa I don't know about? I mean, who else would feel threatened?"

She shook her head. "I have no idea. I can't imagine anyone wanting to close down my bakery. I have a steady and loyal customer base."

"Me, for one." Maurice lifted a tray of eclairs. "These are my favorites." He stared at them for a long moment. "Such a waste," he said as he dumped them into the bag.

Once they'd emptied all the cases, they worked through the kitchen's refrigerators and storage shelves until all the supplies, ingredients and spices were bagged and tossed in the giant bin out back. Through it all, Amelie wrote on a pad clamped to a clipboard, noting items and quantities.

She hung the clipboard on a hook on the wall, looked around and then marched to a small storage room. She emerged with shop towels and a dustmop. "You can start by wiping the flour off all upper surfaces while I follow you with the dust-mop. You can dampen the rags in the sink."

Starting in the front of the shop, they worked side by side, slowly and meticulously removing all traces of flour from the counters, floors and walls.

With hours of work ahead, Maurice hoped to learn more about the pretty baker. "If you don't mind me asking, how long were you and your boyfriend together before he passed?"

CHAPTER 3

AMELIE TURNED from where she'd been working the dirt and dust out of the corner behind the display cabinet. A frown pulled her eyebrows toward the bridge of her nose. "Boyfriend?"

"You said you lost a very dear friend. I assumed he was someone close to you." Maurice swiped his clean rag over the glass display, watching her out of the corner of his eye.

Her frown softened as she thought about Armand. "Oh, he wasn't my boyfriend. He was my mentor—the chef I worked under as a student, and later as his sous chef. We became very close."

"You must have loved him a lot."

"I did. He was more than my teacher. More than my boss. He was like a father to me." She stood still for a moment, her dust mop frozen in the corner. "Armand was a talented chef and an amazing mentor. I would not be half the chef I am today if not for his tutelage. He treated me more like a daughter than any other student." As if she suddenly remembered where she was, she pushed the dust mop around the floor again.

Maurice passed her on his way to rinse the shop rag in the sink. "Didn't Armand have a family of his own?"

Amelie smiled softly. "Yes and no."

"What do you mean?" He paused before turning on the water.

"He was married. I didn't know that for the first year I knew Armand, because his wife lived in California." Her mentor had rarely spoken about his personal life.

"How did you find out he was married?"

"Armand took a couple of days off, saying he had to take care of some business. He came back to the *Chez Benoît* a few days later with a younger version of himself. Armand introduced him as Luis, his son." Her lips twisted into a wry smile. "I didn't know he had a son, much less that he was married, until that moment. Only he wasn't married anymore, because his wife had died and sent his son to live with him in France."

"How old was the son?" Maurice asked as he rinsed the rag in the sink full of soapy water.

"He was seventeen at that time." Her brows drew together. "I felt so bad for both of them. It was a tough time for Armand and for Luis. I became Armand's sounding board when he couldn't relate to his son." Her mentor had opened up about so much he'd kept bottled inside for so long.

"How so?" Maurice wrung out the rag and returned to the counter, near where Amelie worked.

"It's a long story," she said. "Are you sure you want to hear it?"

"It's passing the time," Maurice said. "And I like listening to your voice."

Her cheeks flooded with heat before she turned away to attack another portion of the flour-covered floor. "Luis had lost his mother, had been taken to another continent, to a country he hadn't grown up in and had to live with a father he didn't know. Fortunately, his mother had made sure he spoke French since he had dual citizenship in the US and in France, or it could've been worse."

"Had Armand and his wife divorced?" Maurice asked.

"Apparently not," Amelie said. "He told me that

he and Julia met at a nightclub in Paris when they were both young. He was a young sous chef in Paris. She was there on a student visa, studying art."

Maurice grunted. "Great place to study art with museums like the Louvre, Orsay and the Monet exhibits."

Amelie nodded. "Julia loved art. Armand loved food. Together, they shared their love of Paris. In the process, they fell in love. They'd only known each other for a couple of months when they married. They could barely afford an apartment on what he was making as a sous chef. But they had love." Amelie had finished with the dust mop out front and stood it in a corner. "Are you finished with wiping down the counters and display cases?"

He nodded. "You should inspect. I'm sure your standards are much higher than mine." He rinsed the shop rag in the soapy water and handed it to her. "You'll need this."

She took the cloth and walked through the shop front from the entry door to the display cabinets, armed and ready to pounce on even the slightest smudge or errant flake of flour that Maurice had missed.

After a few minutes, she stood back, shaking

her head. "Well done, my friend. Well done." She grinned. "I couldn't have done better myself."

Maurice's lips spread in a grin. "All the latrines I cleaned with a toothbrush in basic combat training paid off."

"Eww." Amelie grimaced. "Not a good analogy." She drew in a breath and nodded toward the kitchen. "Do you need a break, or are you ready to tackle the kitchen? And no. I'm not issuing you a toothbrush for this effort. The health department inspectors would not be amused."

"I'm ready."

"Then while you start in there, I'll mop this room and then join you."

Maurice helped her fill the mop bucket with a lemon-scented floor cleaner and water. While she mopped, he started on the refrigerators.

Amelie joined him a half an hour later, satisfied that the front of the shop was ready for freshly baked goods and customers.

"Okay," Maurice said, "you can't leave me hanging. I want to hear more about your friend Armand."

Amelie found a clean rag, refilled the sink with warm soapy water, dunked her rag and squeezed out the excess.

"Where was I?" she asked as she worked on the shelves that had held the ingredients.

"Armand and his wife were broke, living on love."

She nodded. "He said they were fine until she got pregnant. He'd just signed on as chef for a struggling restaurant that had just been sold to an investor with big ideas. Armand was working a lot of overtime and was away from Julia for much of her pregnancy. The night she went into labor, he barely made it home in time to take her to the hospital to deliver baby Luis."

"Did she have any difficulties in the delivery?"

Amelie shook her head. "No, but Julia had a hard time recovering. She didn't want to get out of bed. Armand took off so much time helping her that he nearly lost his job. She was homesick for her family and the support system she'd left behind."

"Postpartum depression?" Maurice suggested.

Amelie nodded. "Sounds like it."

"When she finally was able to take care of herself and Luis, Armand threw everything he had into his work, trying to build a name for himself and for the restaurant to justify the owner's investment and make more money to support his family."

Amelie tossed her rag in the sink full of soapy water, grabbed the mop and squeezed out the excess water. As she mopped the corner of the kitchen they'd finished, she continued her story. "He came home one night with the news that a highly regarded food critic had visited the restaurant and had complimented the chef on the food presented. His review would be good in the newspaper the following day. He was so excited about sharing the information with his wife. But when he opened the door, Julia, Luis and all their things were gone, except the empty crib, the highchair and a stroller."

"She went back to California?" Maurice stopped cleaning the stove and straightened.

Amelie's heart pinched hard in her chest. Armand had been so stoic when he'd shared that part of his story with her. He'd completely blamed himself for not seeing her misery. "She left a note that said she was going home to California, because she couldn't raise Luis without help. He could divorce her if he wanted, but she still loved him and wanted him to follow his dream of becoming the best chef in Paris."

"Wow." Maurice shook his head. "He didn't go after her?"

"No." Amelie sighed. "He had a job in Paris, not

in California. Julia and Luis lived with her parents. Armand sent money so that she didn't have to work."

"But he didn't follow her." Maurice shook his head.

"He didn't think he could make it in California. He didn't want to burden her parents by moving in with them while he tried to get his green card and find a job. He'd barely started making a name for himself with the restaurant in Paris. Who would hire him in California?"

"So, she stayed with her folks." Maurice frowned. "Why didn't the parents take Luis when Julia died?"

"They died the year before she did in a massive pileup on the interstate. Julia inherited the house and was digging through their assets when she discovered she had cancer. She didn't tell Armand she was sick until she was in hospice and realized that, as Luis's only living relative, Armand would have to take his son and see him through the rest of his education."

"That had to be hard on Luis as well as Armand."

"Armand was heartbroken. Even after all the years apart, he still loved Julia. He stayed with her and held her hand as she took her last breath."

"And Luis?"

"Grieving. Angry at being whisked off to Paris by his absentee father. I think he blamed Armand for Julia's death, even though he had nothing to do with her cancer. Armand brought him to Paris and enrolled him in an international school that would set him on a path to college at any school of his choice. Between the money Julia's parents left her and the funds Armand set aside for his son's higher education, the boy was set for a strong future."

"I take it Luis didn't settle in very well." Maurice continued wiping the stovetop.

Amelie scrunched her nose. "No. His grades were abysmal. He argued with Armand whenever they were together. Luis limped through his last year in high school and told Armand he had no intention of going to college. Armand tried to get him interested in becoming a chef. He even brought Luis on as a student in his kitchen after he graduated."

"He wasn't interested, was he?"

Amelie shook her head. "Not at all. I tried to help where I could by running interference when they butted heads. I tried to be a friend to Luis since he'd left all his friends behind in California."

"Did it help?"

"A little. But it all seemed a little too late. Especially when his father died. Luis was just shy of twenty-one when Armand passed." Amelie swallowed hard at the lump forming in her throat.

"How did Amand die?" Maurice asked softly.

She gripped the mop tightly and stared at her reflection in the shiny stainless-steel door of the refrigerator. Amelie didn't see herself. She saw Armand lying on the floor of the restaurant kitchen. The early morning light fell across his pale and waxy face. He'd lain face-down, his cheek pressed into a dark, almost black stain on his usually spotless floor. Unmoving. Not breathing. "The *médecin légiste* report stated that he'd had a heart attack. When he fell, he hit his head on the corner of the counter."

"Who found him?" Maurice asked.

She turned to face him. His face blurred through her tears. "Me."

Maurice set his rag aside and crossed to her. He took the mop from her hands and set it aside. Then he pulled her into his arms. "I'm sorry."

"For what?" she whispered.

"I'm sorry you had to be the one who found him." He held her close, stroking her hair. "It's hard to see someone you love...like that."

She wrapped her arms around his waist. "I was in a state of denial. It couldn't be real. It wasn't

Armand. He wasn't dead." She leaned her cheek against his shoulder.

"Was that what you were thinking about on the dance floor?"

She nodded. "It was three years ago last night that he died. Each year, it seems a little easier to make it through the day. I was feeling guilty that the memories are fading. That the pain of his death is becoming more bearable. It shouldn't, should it?" She leaned back and looked up into his face.

He shook his head. "Life goes on. Those of us lucky enough to live have to keep going. Truth is, none of us is getting out of this alive. We just don't know when our number is up. When our time is up. We can't stop living because someone we loved died."

Amelie frowned. "You know."

He nodded.

"Who did you lose?"

"A couple of my brothers in arms, my mother and father," he paused for only a second, "and my fiancée."

Amelie's eyes widened. "Oh, Maurice. I should be comforting you, not the other way around."

His mouth quirked on one corner. "In a way, you are." Tightening his arms around her briefly, he pressed his lips to her forehead. "Maybe misery does love company. And maybe through shared sorrow we can find our way to happiness." He set her at arm's length. "And maybe we will get more work done and make a brighter future if we aren't wallowing in the past." He tipped the mop handle into her hands.

When she wrapped her hands around it, he didn't release it. Maurice stared down into her eyes. "I'm not pushing you away, Amelie. But I mean it, wallowing won't do justice to those who have passed. I know. I did it long enough. I sank so deep in sadness, I wanted to end my own life."

Amelie gasped. "You?"

He nodded. "Me. That's when I finally pulled myself up by the bootstraps and got on with the business of living. My friends, my parents and my fiancée wouldn't have wanted me to stop living because they had. They would've wanted me to live my life to its fullest. For them. For me."

Amelie nodded. "That's what I've tried to do. After Armand died, I tried to fill Armand's shoes as chef. The restaurant owner felt Chez Benoît wouldn't survive without its namesake and head chef. They closed the restaurant for good. I couldn't stay in Paris without a job, so I had to come back to the States. I went to work in New Orleans, as it was as close to home as I could be and still work as the chef Armand trained me to be. Not just a *pâtissière*."

"Why didn't that work?"

"I was close to home but by myself. When my apartment was broken into, I realized New Orleans wasn't for me. Too much city for a lone woman." She snorted softly. "That might make me a coward, but I get where Julia was coming from. I couldn't do it on my own. I needed a support system of people I cared about and who cared about me. I had that in Paris with Armand until he died. After the break-in here, I realize," she waved a hand to the side, "my people are here. In Bayou Mambaloa."

"And you've done very well if your happy customers are anything to go on." He stroked her hand holding the mop handle. "Any regrets?"

She drew in a deep breath and let it out. "Luis."

Maurice frowned. "What happened with Luis after his father died?"

"I was with him at the funeral. Before the restaurant closed, I helped him organize his father's estate. He was clueless. Not that I had much of an idea. When the owners of Chez Benoît announced they were closing, I asked Luis to come with me to New Orleans. He chose to go back to

California, where he still had some friends from when he'd been in high school."

"How is he doing?" Maurice asked. "Do you keep in touch?"

Amelie gave Maurice a twisted smile. "I'm sure if it were up to Luis, we would have fallen out of touch. But I make it a point to call him every month."

"And?"

She sighed. "He's living on his inheritance. Thankfully, Armand had it placed in a trust where he only gets so much each month until he turns thirty-five. Then it will all go to him. Otherwise, I'm not sure how he would've handled it."

"Did he get a job? Go back to school?"

"He went back to school as soon as he returned to California. I'm not sure what he was studying, but he said he was making good grades and was making friends. Last month, he said he'd gotten a part-time job at a restaurant, of all places. This from a guy who wouldn't let his world-renowned chef father teach him what he knew."

"Sounds like he might be getting his head on straight."

"I hope so. He's not my son, but Armand would've been glad to know I didn't abandon him completely. That someone was looking out for him."

"You're a good person, Amelie," Maurice said and released his hold on the mop handle.

"I feel like I'd have been better if I could've convinced Luis to come with me."

"But you can't tell a young man anything," Maurice said. "I know. I was a young man once. No one could tell me anything. I had to learn for myself."

Her eyebrows shot upward. "You?"

He nodded. "There were so many times I wished I'd listened to my parents. *After* I was in trouble. Or my drill sergeant. Again, *after* I was in trouble and doing a million pushups for some stupid stunt I thought was a good idea at the time."

Amelie laughed. "Stubborn much?"

"Too much."

She sighed. "I usually call Luis around this time every year, not so much to remind him that his father died at this time, but because thinking of Armand reminds me to call and check on his son."

"What's keeping you?"

She stared out a window at the gray light of dawn, just barely making the world visible outside. "It's too early here. It'll be even earlier in California. But I will. Later. For now, I need to finish cleaning and get on the road to New Orleans to buy supplies."

They went back to work, finishing up as the sun rose.

Amelie followed Maurice as he carried the mop bucket out the back door. They were just in time to watch the sunrise set Bayou Mambaloa on fire with all the reds, oranges and yellows imaginable.

"This is why I love it here so much. It's not just the people who fill my life, it's the peace and beauty of the bayou," she said softly.

When Maurice cocked an eyebrow in her direction, Amelie laughed. "Okay, having my bakery vandalized isn't so peaceful, but the bayou does not disappoint with the show it's putting on this morning."

Maurice tossed the water across the back parking lot and turned to face her.

Amelie smiled. "Thank you for helping me get the shop back in order. And thank you for being here for me."

He turned the bucket upside down, straightened and gave her a dip of his head. "My pleasure."

Amelie wanted to say more, but her cell phone rang at that moment. She glanced down and frowned.

"Who is it?" Maurice asked.

"Luis," she said. "He never calls me. And why is he calling so early?" She answered the call. "Luis? Is everything all right?"

"Amelie," Luis's voice sounded in her ear. "I hope I didn't wake you."

"Not at all," she said, her gaze on Maurice, a frown pulling at her brow. "What's wrong?"

He laughed. "Nothing's wrong. It's just that I'm in New Orleans and hoped I could come see you."

CHAPTER 4

BEFORE THEY HEADED for New Orleans, Maurice opted for a quick shower and change of clothing at the boarding house he'd been living in since arriving in Bayou Mambaloa. So many of his team had already transitioned out of the boarding house after finding love and commitment with some of the town's residents.

Maurice had been looking at local real estate but had yet to commit. None of the homes LaShawnda Jones, his realtor, had shown him had felt like *home*. Not that he knew what that felt like anymore. Growing up a military brat, every place they'd moved had always felt like home. He'd never thought any differently or questioned it.

Looking at houses in Bayou Mambaloa, Maurice couldn't find that natural, let your guard down and get comfortable feeling he'd had as a child. Watching his buddies fall in love and establish homes with their women was beginning to make something very clear.

Home wasn't a place or building. It was who you were with.

Maurice thought he'd found that someone he could make a home with when he'd fallen for Sandy. Her death had hit him hard. Since then, he hadn't been interested in finding a home or even a house.

The boarding house the Brotherhood Protectors had purchased was a transitional place where new recruits could live until they found permanent lodging.

Not having found permanent lodging, Maurice had stayed longer than temporarily. He'd only just started looking for a place of his own after living in the boarding house for nearly two years.

Amelie took the van to the gas station to fuel up while Maurice showered and changed.

He was waiting for her when she drove up outside the boarding house. Leaving his truck, he joined her in the bakery van.

As they drove into the city, Amelie's hands tightened on the steering wheel, her lips pressing into a tight line.

"Does driving in traffic make you tense?" he asked.

She nodded.

'I'd think that after living in Paris you'd get used to a big city."

She snorted. "In Paris, we walked everywhere. When I lived in New Orleans, I stayed in an apartment not too far from where I worked. I didn't have to drive in the traffic very often. It's just another reason I like being home in Bayou Mambaloa."

"Are you nervous about seeing Luis?" Maurice asked.

"No, not really," Amelie said. "It's just the first time he's come to see me since I moved back to the US." She frowned. "Why now?"

"Is it a little weird that it's right after your bakery was broken into?"

She shrugged and drove the van into a parking lot near Bourbon Street. "I'm probably chasing shadows. It just seems to be a bit of a coincidence."

"I never believe in coincidence," Maurice said.

"Then it's nothing." Amelie pulled into a space and turned off the engine. "A lot of people come to New Orleans. He's no different. It's an interesting city with lots to offer."

"What about the fact that your apartment in this city was vandalized as well?"

"That was nearly two years ago. I doubt there's a connection between then and now."

"Did they take anything in that first break-in?"

"Just my electronics—a TV and a handheld speaker. I didn't have much."

"A typical break-in with the intent to take anything they can sell in a pawn shop." He shook his head. "Which doesn't make sense that your bakery was broken into, but whoever did it didn't take anything. He could've gone after the cash in the register, or even the cash register, or the television in your apartment."

"But he didn't." Amelie shifted into park, turned off the engine and turned to Maurice. "You don't have to come to this meeting with Luis."

"Do you prefer to go alone?" He tilted his head. "Or are you trying to give me a break?"

"No and yes," she answered with a crooked smile. "I'm giving you an out."

"If you're okay with me tagging along, that's what I'd like to do."

"Okay. Then, after lunch, we can go pick up all the supplies I'll need. Shouldn't take too long since I called in the order to my supplier."

They left the parking garage and walked to

Mambo's on Bourbon Street, the Cajun-American restaurant Amelie had assured Maurice had a great Cajun menu.

Maurice held the door for Amelie, admiring the scent of her shampoo as she passed by. She'd showered and changed into clean clothing after they'd finished cleaning the bakery and setting her apartment to rights.

Inside the restaurant, Amelie glanced around at the tables filled with the lunch crowd of tourists and locals.

A hand rose from a table in the far corner.

"Ah," Amelie smiled. "There he is."

Maurice followed her as she weaved her way through the tables, stopping at the one where a young man with brown hair and brown eyes sat.

As Amelie approached, the man got up.

"Luis," Amelie smiled and hugged him. "I'm so glad to see you. It's been way too long."

"You're right. Far too long." Luis hugged her and stepped back. "It's good to see you, too."

Amelie turned to Maurice. "Maurice, this is Luis Benoît, my mentor and friend, Armand's son." She turned to Luis. "Luis, I hope you don't mind that I brought my friend Maurice. We have to pick up supplies for the bakery after lunch, and he offered to help."

Luis shook hands with Maurice, demonstrating a strong grip for such a young man. "Pleasure to meet you," Luis said with very little French accent.

"Nice to meet you," Maurice said and pulled out a chair for Amelie. "Amelie tells me you two worked together in Paris."

Luis's gaze met Amelie's. "Amelie worked. I'm not sure I was much help in my father's restaurant."

"You were a big help." Amelie settled in her chair.

Once Luis and Maurice took their seats, a waiter appeared to take their drink orders.

Maurice asked for water. Luis ordered a soft drink, and Amelie opted for sweet tea.

"I grew up in Louisiana," Amelie said. "Sweet tea, Cajun cuisine and my friends were what I missed most when I was in Paris."

Luis smiled as he lifted the menu. "I remember when you introduced me to sweet tea. It was shortly after I moved in with my father."

"I didn't make it too often. I really had to work on my tea palate to even barely appreciate flavored teas. Your father helped me there, along with taste, type and pairings of wine." She sighed and leaned closer. "How are you, Luis? How are you liking living back in California?"

The waiter returned with the drinks before Luis could respond.

Once he'd set the glasses on the table, he took their orders.

"I'll have shrimp etouffee," Amelie said. "My favorite."

"Excellent choice." Maurice tilted his head. "I also like a good gumbo. That's what I'll have."

Luis ordered a shrimp po' boy.

After the waiter left with their orders, Luis drew in a deep breath. "As for California...I thought I'd like to be back where I grew up, but nothing's the same."

"It rarely is, going back to your hometown," Amelie said. "With the exception of Bayou Mambaloa," she said with a smile. "Most of my friends were still there or had come back. Was that not the case for you?"

Luis shook his head. "Friends I'd known in high school had either moved out of the state to find jobs or were already married with kids on the way. Though I have my father's trust payments, they aren't enough to cover the cost of living. I got a full-time job at a restaurant." His lips twisted. "As a dishwasher, which wasn't all bad. I've done that before, working in my father's restaurant in Paris. It was really the only job I could get."

At this point, Luis paused.

Amelie didn't prompt or make a comment. She let the young man continue at his own pace.

Maurice appreciated her patience. He could tell Luis was struggling to get it all out.

"It wasn't enough," Luis said. "I didn't tell you this, but a year ago, I enrolled in culinary school."

Amelie's eyes rounded. "Oh, Luis. That's wonderful." Her brow dipped a moment later. "But why didn't you tell me?"

He looked away. "You and my father tried hard to get me to learn the craft, and all I did was push back. I didn't want to do what everyone expected. I wanted to have a choice in what career I pursued."

"And?" Amelie sat on the edge of her seat, her eyes alight.

Luis sighed. "Yes, there are recipes you have to learn and follow. Yes, there was a lot to learn about meats, cuts, spices, heat and so much more. I also learned there was room for creativity. That making wonderful food was an art, like making music or painting a picture. I finally understood what my father was always trying to tell me."

"You have to have a passion for the culinary arts…?"

Luis nodded. "Or you'll never be a chef. You'll be a cook."

Amelie nodded, a smile spreading across her face. "Your father would've loved to hear you say all that."

"Yeah, I'm sorry he didn't live long enough for me to pull my head out and learn this about myself."

"So, how much longer do you have in culinary school?" Maurice asked.

"I finished the course I was in and applied for an internship here in New Orleans at Maison Belle and got in. I start as an apprentice in a week."

Amelie clapped her hands. "That's where I worked before I moved back home to Bayou Mambaloa."

"I remembered," Luis said with a smile. Then his brow dipped. "I don't understand why you left to open a bakery in a small town. You have skills equal to my father's. Seems like a waste of talent."

Amelie shook her head. "I still use a wide range of my skills as a caterer when needed, but I love the pace in the small town, and I've always loved baking. The best part is that I have a great support system with my friends."

Luis nodded. "That means a lot. I hope I can find that here in New Orleans."

The waiter returned with their meals.

Maurice inhaled the rich scents of spices.

For the next few minutes, silence descended as they ate.

Luis set his po'boy down and drank some of his soda. "Something strange occurred before I left California."

Amelie swallowed a bite of food and asked, "What's that?"

"I had a visitor come to my apartment. It was a man with a German accent. He said his name was Fredrick Schulz."

Amelie tilted her head. "What did he want?"

"He said he was studying wealthy French families that had survived WWII and where they were now. He wanted to know about my father and his family history. He asked if my father's family had managed to escape with any of their antiquities, art, journals or diaries."

"What did you tell him?" Amelie asked.

"I really don't know much about my father's family history. Just that his family was displaced from their home in Paris during World War II and didn't return until France was liberated." He lifted his sandwich and stared at it for a moment. "When I had the chance to ask more about my family history, I wasn't interested. Now that I can't ask, I'd like to know more. As it is, I know very few specifics about his siblings, parents, or extended family. I know more about my mother's side of the family because we lived together in California."

Amelie took a sip of her sweet tea and set the glass on the table. "Your father was very occupied with his restaurant, but on the occasional day off, he'd have me over to dinner and talk about his past. His mother and father told him stories about the beautiful estate they'd lived in before the German occupation. When Germans entered France in May of 1940, his parents had had to pack up their belongings, anything of value and escape before the reached Paris. In early June, they left their home in the middle of the night to avoid detection. They went from being wealthy Parisians to hiding in the countryside until they found their way to a ship that took them to the United States."

"Where in the US?" Luis asked.

Maurice wanted to know as well, curious about Amelie's mentor.

Amelie smiled. "Right here in New Orleans. They spent five years here in New Orleans. His father found work in the shipping industry, while his mother worked in a bakery. His parents' love of good food inspired Armand's desire to pursue the culinary arts."

"I always wondered where he'd gotten his inspiration," Luis said.

"Did you know your father was born here?" Amelie asked.

"I did not." Luis's lips twisted. "There's so much I didn't know or want to learn about my father. I do now."

She gave him a brief smile. "You had a lot to deal with your mother's passing and leaving behind the only world you knew to live with a father you'd rarely seen."

"I was so angry." Luis shook his head. "At everyone and everything. I was even angry at my mother for dying, leaving me no choice but to go live with my father. I was angry at him because he was alive and my mother wasn't."

"And now?" Amelie asked softly.

"I didn't give him much of a chance." He looked away. "I didn't know how much I missed until he was gone."

"Sometimes, it takes a tragedy to make you realize what you really want in life," Maurice said. "And what you're missing."

Luis met Maurice's gaze. "Exactly. After my father died, I was in such a hurry to return to my old life, but I didn't try to hold onto anything that meant anything to him or his family."

Amelie nodded. "We were both left in shock by his death. When the restaurant closed shortly after,

I wasn't much help. I had to clear out. My work visa ended."

"I wish I'd kept some of his more personal items. He didn't have any artwork or antiques, that I know of." Luis pulled a pocket watch out of his pocket. "He didn't keep journals or anything of real value, besides this pocket watch he said his father passed down to him." He flipped it open. "It doesn't even work."

"I'm sure you can find someone to repair it here in New Orleans," Maurice said.

Luis's lips quirked upward on the corners. "It's strange. My father gave it to me the night before he died. He knew it didn't work, but said it was his father's before him, that I should keep it safe. It meant a lot to him and to his father." Luis flipped the cover open. "It has an inscription on it I haven't been able to figure out." He passed the watch across the table to Amelie. "It's just numbers. Any clue what they might mean?"

Amelie frowned down at the numbers engraved on the inside cover. "I have no idea."

"May I?" Maurice asked.

"Please," Luis said. "I thought maybe it was a birthdate or the day the watch was given as a gift, but it has too many numbers."

Maurice pulled out his cell phone and snapped

several photos of the watch and the numbers inside it. "There are too many numbers for it to be one set of coordinates and not enough for two sets."

"Yeah. That's what I figured. What group of numbers would've been important to my grandfather, who lived in Paris? I thought, for a moment, they were the numbers tattooed on the arms of my father's French neighbors who'd been sent to Nazi death camps."

"Makes more sense." Amelie stared at the numbers. "You say your father didn't have any keepsakes or journals. Did you keep any of his old photos?"

"That's what the German asked." Luis shook his head. "He had a photo of the three of us when I was a child." He smiled. "My mother and father were so young in that picture. And there were several black-and-white photos of his parents. Now that I've seen the St. Louis Cathedral, I know they took one of those pictures here in New Orleans."

"I remember he had that photo in a frame on an end table in his flat in Paris," Amelie said. "That's when he told me they'd moved to New Orleans near the beginning of World War II. As soon as the war was over and it was safe to return, they packed up and moved back to Paris." Amelie frowned. "Did you keep the photos he had on the bookshelf?"

"I kept all the photos," Luis said with a shrug. "It was pretty much all I had left of my father's."

Amelie's eyes narrowed. "Those were pictures of his parents before the war, taken in their home. He pointed them out, talking about the beautiful furnishings and paintings they had on the walls. So much of what they had in their home was also passed down from generation to generation. When they returned from the States, all of that was gone —their home, the furnishings, everything they hadn't taken with them. They had to start over. Your father said they didn't have much, but they slowly rebuilt their lives. Your grandmother's baking helped keep a roof over their heads. Your grandfather, like you, got a job washing dishes in a fancy restaurant. He soon apprenticed under the chef and eventually opened his own restaurant."

"The Chez Benoît." Luis sighed. "And now that's gone, as well."

"Who knows," Amelie said. "If you work hard and learn from your mentors, one day you might open your own restaurant."

Luis laughed. "I'm just starting and still in the chief bottle-washer stage of my career."

"You have more of your father in you than you know," Amelie said. "You'll do well as long as you have the passion for creating beautiful, flavorful cuisine."

"Thank you," Luis said. "It means a lot to me to hear you say that. I feel like I didn't leave you on the best of terms. For the years we worked together, you were nothing but nice and helpful. I was a jerk and pushed back every time you tried to show me something or when my father tried to teach me." Luis's eyes brightened. "I'll have you know that I finally mastered *Soufflé au Fromage*. It was so light and tasted so good, I truly believe my father would've been proud."

Amelie nodded. "He would've loved everything about it." She glanced at her watch and blinked. "Wow. The time has flown. I'm really sorry that I can't stay longer. I have an appointment with my supplier in twenty minutes. If I didn't need the supplies so badly, I'd love to stay and talk more." She glanced toward Maurice.

"I'm finished," he said, having polished off his amazing shrimp okra gumbo. "Ready whenever you are."

Amelie pushed to her feet. "Luis, I'm happy you'll be closer, and I hope you like working for

Maison Belle. I loved it. The staff was easy to work with and loved what they did."

Luis stood and hugged Amelie. "I'm glad you made time to come see me. I feel like you're the only family I have. I promise to be better about keeping in touch."

She took his hands. "I'm happy you're finding what inspires you. Since you don't start for another week, come out to Bayou Mambaloa. Stay with me. My apartment is small, but you could always sleep on the sofa."

"If you need a little more room, I'm sure we could put you up in the local boarding house," Maurice offered.

Luis nodded. "I have a few things to do to get settled, but it shouldn't take long. And I don't know anyone here yet. So, yes, I'd like that. Is tomorrow too soon?"

Amelie grinned. "Never too soon. I might even put you to work."

"I'm up for that as well," Luis said. "I'll see you then."

Amelie insisted on paying the bill on the way out.

"Would you like me to drive?" Maurice asked.

"Actually, I'd love it if you would," she said with

a relaxed smile. She handed him the keys and slid into the passenger seat.

Maurice climbed into the driver's seat, keyed the address into his smartphone, started the engine and pulled out of the parking garage into the midday traffic.

"It was really nice to see Luis," Amelie said. "I was worried about him after Armand's death. Losing both parents when he's still so young is hard."

"He seems to have found purpose."

"And he's training to be a chef." She nodded. "Armand would've been so proud. Hell, he would've been proud of any profession his son went into."

"Like most parents, he would've been glad his son found something he liked doing and went after it."

Amelie stared out the windshield, her smile making Maurice smile.

Something Luis had mentioned tugged at Maurice's thoughts. "I wonder what the German guy was looking for by calling on Luis?"

"I thought that was weird, too." Amelie's brow furrowed, wiping away her contented smile. "Seems odd that a German would be researching wealthy French families of WWII."

"Luis said he specifically asked about antiquities and art."

Amelie nodded. "As well as journals or diaries."

"The Nazi's confiscated a lot of famous artwork from all over Europe. Not all of it has been found and returned to the families or institutions where it belonged."

"Armand did say that his folks packed up all their valuables and escaped into the night." Amelie glanced toward Maurice. "Do you think they took their artwork and antiquities with them?"

Maurice shrugged. "Maybe. If they did, they might've sold them to pay for their passage on a ship. Or they could've sold them to keep a roof over their heads when they had to start over in New Orleans and then in Paris when they returned."

"I spent enough time in Armand's Paris apartment to know he didn't have any artwork or antiques." Amelie's brow dipped further. "Other than with his work as a chef, he was very much a minimalist."

"If his folks fled with their valuables, could those valuables still be missing?"

"Is there any way to find out what famous artwork or antiques a particular family might have owned before the beginning of WWII?"

Maurice shrugged. "I don't know. But I know someone who might find out if Armand's relatives owned anything of significance. We have a computer guy at Brotherhood Protectors headquarters in Montana who can scan the web for any recorded history of Armand's family. Maybe Swede could find out if they owned anything others might want to find. It could be the German has already done his homework and knows of something they had that hasn't resurfaced, and he's trying to chase it down."

"You think that's possible?"

"If there's any information on Armand's family, Swede will find it."

"What about the pocket watch?" Amelie glanced across at Maurice. "Do you think that's one of the antiquities the German was looking for?"

"I'll send the photo of the watch to Swede. If it's worth anything, he'll let us know."

Amelie pulled out her cell phone and keyed a text message. "I'm asking Luis to snap copies of the photos he kept. The ones of his grandparents, before they had to abandon their home, were taken inside their house. Maybe there's a painting or antique in the background that could give us an idea of what they had."

"Good idea. That might help Swede." Maurice followed the directions to the supply house and backed into the loading dock. As he shifted into park, Amelie's phone chirped with an incoming message.

"Luis said he'd send the pictures when he gets back to his apartment," Amelie said.

"What did he say about your reason for wanting them?"

Amelie grimaced. "I didn't tell him exactly why I wanted them, other than to say I wanted copies to remember Armand by. Everything we've talked about is..."

"Conjecture." Maurice nodded. "I get it. When we find out more, we can let him in on it."

"Or, if we don't find anything, he won't be waiting around hoping we will and be disappointed." Amelie drew in a breath and let it out. "Armand was always so particular about his cuisine and the presentation. I found it odd that his own home was sparse and unadorned."

"Maybe because it wasn't home to him," Maurice suggested. "Not after his wife left anyway."

Amelie nodded. "I got that feeling. The only time he seemed happy was when he was creating cuisine at the restaurant. Anywhere else, he appeared pensive, even sad. Once, we were walking along a boulevard in Paris on our way to purchase spices, when he slowed and stared at a store for so long, I asked what was wrong. He said the store used to be a bistro. It was a place he and Julia had shared stories about their lives over a cup of coffee or espresso."

"He must've loved her very much," Maurice said.

"In his way, he did." Amelie pushed open her door. "Here comes the dock worker."

Amelie went into full-on bakery-business-owner mode and supervised the loading of the supplies she'd ordered, going over the list, item by item, to ensure the entire order was satisfied.

While he waited, Maurice stepped away from the loading dock and called Swede.

"Swede here," he answered on the second ring.

"Swede, Maurice Boucher, out of the Bayou branch."

"Maurice, good to hear from you. What can I do for you?"

"I'm working with Amelie Aubert in Bayou Mambaloa."

"I heard that you were. She had a break-in last night."

"That's right."

"Have they caught the guy?"

"No," Maurice said. "We met with Luis Benoît, the son of Amelie's former mentor, a French chef by the name of Armand Benoît. Luis had a man with a German accent, who identified himself as Fredrick Schulz, asking him about his father's family, supposedly researching wealthy French families during WWII and where they are now."

"Interesting that a German was asking about French families," Swede commented. "But go on."

"I need you to do your magic and find out anything you can about Schulz. Who is he? Who does he work for? Basically, is he legit?"

"Fredrick Schulz," Swede repeated. "Got it."

"Also, look up French chef Armand Benoît's parents. Who were they, and did they own any valuable artwork or antiquities that might've been lost or disappeared during WWII?"

"On it," Swede responded.

"One more thing…" Maurice put the phone on speaker, pulled up the photo of the pocket watch and forwarded it to Swede's number. "I just sent you a photograph of a pocket watch Armand gave to his son the day before he died."

"I have it," Swede acknowledged.

"Check it out. Is it worth anything? And if you have any idea what the numbers are on the inside of the cover, we'd like to know. It's got us stumped."

"I'll do what I can."

"Thanks, Swede," Maurice said. "Out here."

"Out here," Swede said and ended the call.

Once he'd finished the call, Maurice helped load the items after Amelie checked them off the list. He admired her professionalism and kindness when working with the dock laborer. When the items were loaded, she shook the man's hand and thanked him before closing the back door of the van.

Maurice opened the passenger door for her. "You don't mind if I drive?"

She shook her head. "Not if you don't mind driving."

"I'd be honored." He handed her up into the van and closed the door.

Maurice shifted into gear and drove out of the loading dock. "Do we need to stop anywhere else before heading back to Bayou Mambaloa?"

Amelie leaned her head back against the seat. "No. They were able to hook me up with everything I needed. I'm ready to get back, unload and get set up for tomorrow."

"Are you going to open tomorrow?"

She drew in a deep breath. If I can get some

sleep tonight so that I'm not the walking dead at three-thirty in the morning, I'll open on time. I can't guarantee a full list of what I usually prepare, but I'll have what most people order. And coffee."

"Sounds like a plan. I'll help however I can."

She leaned her head to the side to look his way. "You really don't have to, you know. If they've caught the vandal, there will be no need for you to stay."

Maurice shot her a pointed look. "Have they caught the vandal?"

Amelie glanced down at her phone.

"Wouldn't Shelby have called you if they had?"

Her lips twisted. "Yes."

"You could call and ask her if they've found them to make certain," Maurice offered softly.

Amelie lifted her cell phone, paused and lowered it. "No. Shelby would call if they'd caught him."

"So, until we know more about the guy who trashed your place, I'm not leaving you or these supplies without protection. You've spent too much time cleaning and too much money on new supplies, along with worrying about your business, for me to feel right walking away. I'll be at the bakery tonight. If that means sleeping on the floor to guard the goods, or staying awake all night, I'm there. Unless it's me you don't want to protect you. I can send someone else from my team."

Amelie's gaze met his. "No. No, it's not you. I just..." She sighed, "I don't like being a bother to you."

He reached across and took her hand in his. "You're not a bother. I'm fascinated by how wonderfully you've rebounded after having your building violated. You're a true professional. And you're cute with flour on your nose."

Amelie reached up automatically to touch her fingers to her nose.

Maurice chuckled. "Not now, but earlier this morning."

Her smile returned, brightening Maurice's day. His own smile joined hers as he drove out of New Orleans and back home. To Bayou Mambaloa.

CHAPTER 5

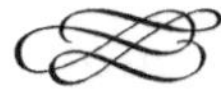

AMELIE MUST HAVE FALLEN asleep on the way back to the bakery. She didn't wake until a hand slipped beneath her thighs and another slid behind her back and lifted her.

She blinked her eyes open and stared up at the blue sky, wondering where the hell she was and why she was pressed up against a wall of muscle.

"What...? Where...?" she murmured as she fought her way out of the fog of exhaustion.

"We're here at the bakery. I'm carrying you up to your apartment so you can sleep," Maurice stared down at her, his dark brown eyes smiling down at her as he climbed the stairs to the upper level of the bakery building. He stopped at the top and nodded. "The team has been here to reinforce your doorframe and install a new deadbolt." He reached out with a shiny new key, inserted it into the lock and pushed the door open.

"How did you get the key?" she asked, her voice sounding groggy and foreign to her ears.

"I made a call while you were asleep. Remy had a couple of the guys reinforce your doorframe and install a new deadbolt. I stopped at the boat factory for the key, and here we are. You slept the entire time." Maurice stepped inside.

Amelie lifted her head and stared around at the small apartment. Her apartment. Her personal space that had been violated.

For a moment, she expected to see it as she had right after the break-in. Fortunately, everything was clean and in its proper place from all the work they'd done early that morning.

God, she was tired.

Her first instinct was to lean into Maurice's strength and let him shoulder the burden for a few more minutes.

When he carried her across the small living area to her bedroom door, her body heated. Completely involuntarily. A strong, handsome man carrying her to her bedroom awakened all kinds of possibilities inside her, bringing her to an abrupt state of awareness and fully awake.

Though she was content... No. Comfortable...

No, that wasn't the word. Although she was suddenly, startlingly aware of the man holding her in his arms, she fought to remain calm and determine how she could extricate herself without touching him any more than she already was—before she succumbed to the rising desire spreading like wildfire throughout her body.

"I'm awake," she squeaked and tried again in a more measured tone. "I'm awake. You can put me down."

"Are you sure?" Maurice asked. "You slept all the way from New Orleans, through the stop I made at the boat factory and me carrying you up the stairs. I think you could use more sleep before you tackle unloading the van, organizing all the supplies and prepping for your O-dark-thirty rise to bake the goods to feed the masses."

Amelie closed her eyes for a moment, really wanting to stay right where she was.

The only other place she'd rather be was in bed, naked with this man.

Her eyes popped open at the thought, and heat flooded her neck, rushing up into her cheeks. "No, really. I'm wide awake."

At least, she was now because she was shocked to consciousness with the realization that she was having hot half-awake dreams about the man still holding her in his arms.

"Seriously, you can put me down. I'm well and truly awake."

He paused in her bedroom doorway. "Are you sure? I could unload all the supplies, put those that need to be cool in the refrigerator and the rest on the counters until you tell me where to store them."

"No. I need to be there." She gave him a crooked smile. "The nap helped. I should have the energy to see this through. And the sooner I get started, the sooner I can go to bed."

Maurice nodded. "Okay. You've convinced me." He lowered her legs until her feet touched the floor.

When she swayed, he slipped his hand around her waist and held her until she steadied.

Once Amelie had her feet firmly beneath her, she forced foggy thoughts to coalesce into the tasks ahead.

"I need to bring all the supplies out of the van and place them on the countertops. I'll separate the ingredients I'll need for tomorrow morning's breakfast crowd and store the rest."

"If you think you're up to it," Maurice said, "I'm ready to get started."

Amelie was far from ready. She needed a really good night's rest to make up for the lack of sleep the night before. But if she wanted to get her baked goods prepared on time for the morning crowd, she had to make the impossible possible and get it all done before the clock struck nine—her version of Cinderella's midnight.

"You have to be beyond tired," Maurice said as he stepped back and let his arm drop to his side.

"I got a nap. You have to be dead on your feet," she shot back at him, swaying a little without his strong arm supporting her.

"I've lost more sleep and still functioned," Maurice admitted.

"I might not have performed in a high-intensity battle where lives were on the line, but I've done everything I could to get a wedding reception, complete with flowers, place cards, bar tenders and a five-course meal for the guests planned, prepared and presented in under thirty-six hours." Amelie grimaced. "I do not in any way want to diminish the sacrifices of our American military, but I do understand stress, killer deadlines and making the deadline no matter what it takes."

"Okay, then," Maurice said. "Let's get this show on the road."

"Give me two minutes to splash water on my

face and freshen up. If I'm not out by then, come in with coffee and a cattle prod to get me moving." She turned away and spun back. "Just kidding. I'll be out in two minutes. No cattle prod required."

"Thank God," Maurice said. "I have a moral code that will not allow me to use a cattle prod on a woman, no matter how difficult she might be."

"You own a cattle prod?" Amelie asked.

"Actually, I don't," Maurice said. "I'd never use one on another person. I wouldn't even like to use it on cattle."

"Good to know," she said with a grin. "Doesn't own a cattle prod and is empathetic toward animals." She winked. "I'll be right back."

Maurice stepped back as Amelie closed her bedroom door.

For a long moment, she stared at the door, wanting to open it again and sink into his arms. He was all hard muscles and warm skin, sexy as hell and strong. He'd carried her all the way up the stairs to her apartment. She was no featherweight.

Two minutes. She had two minutes to get a grip, tamp down her wildly beating heart and get to work.

Amelie spun on her heels, hurried into her bathroom and splashed water on her face, hoping to cool the heat rushing through her body. She could still feel his hands on her thighs and behind her back and the hard plains of his chest against her cheek. She had to remind herself that he was there to protect her in case the vandal came back, not to satisfy her every naked fantasy.

At that thought, she splashed more water on her face. It was doing nothing to quench the fire coursing through her veins. She gave up, ran a brush through her tangled hair, pulled it back in a tight ponytail and secured it with a scrunchie at the back of her head.

After she straightened her blouse, she gave herself a glance in the mirror and shrugged. She didn't have time to dab concealer on the dark shadows beneath her eyes or add a little color to her pale cheeks. Every day her business closed impacted the bottom line. That meant the difference between being able to pay for the supplies she'd just put on her credit card and the rent and utilities it took to keep the bakery doors open.

At exactly two minutes from the moment she'd closed her bedroom door, she opened it.

Her heart fluttered at the sight of Maurice standing at the window overlooking Main Street. His broad shoulders filled the room, making it seem much smaller than when she was there alone.

Smaller and warmer. Or was she the one who was warmer?

Amelie shook herself, squared her shoulders and marched through the living area. "Ready?"

He turned with a smile that melted her knees. "Ready." He held out his hand.

She automatically reached for his.

Instead of curling his fingers around hers, he laid a key in her palm. "Hang onto that. It's the key to your new lock."

She wrapped her finger around it, shocked at the pang of disappointment that made her chest tighten.

What had she expected? Just because a man had carried her up a set of stairs didn't mean anything. He was just being nice.

Amelie shoved the key into the pocket of her jeans, pasted a smile on her face and started past Maurice.

He followed her to the door, opened it for her and waited on the landing outside for her to lock it with the new key.

Once she'd pocketed the key again, she turned to start down the stairs.

Maurice reached for her hand and walked down beside her, holding her hand all the way.

Warmth spread through Amelie, making her steps lighter and the tasks ahead of her less daunting.

Between the two of them, they unloaded the supplies from the van into the kitchen.

Amelie quickly sorted through the boxes, bags and bottles of ingredients, giving Maurice guidance on where to store them.

Once she had everything in place and the ingredients for the bread and pastries that the bakery sold most, she stopped to look around with a satisfied smile. "There is one good thing that's come out of the break-in."

Maurice placed a bucket of cooking oil on the floor next to another just like it and straightened. "Oh, yeah? What?"

Her smile broadened. "This place is sparkling clean." She turned her smile on Maurice. "I couldn't have done it without you."

"I'm betting you would've done just fine without me, but thanks. It's been a learning experience. I never knew there was so much going on behind the scenes. I'll have a greater appreciation for my morning éclair and coffee."

Amelie turned to the workbench where she'd left out the ingredients she needed for the next day's baked goods. "Now to make up the dough for bread, bagels, eclairs and donuts."

Maurice shook his head. "Surely, you have time to grab a bite to eat before diving in."

"I can't spare the time it takes to cook a meal or wait for it at a restaurant." She tied an apron over her clothing and pulled a net cap over her head, tucking in her ponytail. "Lunch was enough. But if you're hungry, you don't have to stick around."

A knock sounded at the back door of the kitchen.

Amelie crossed the floor to answer.

Maurice beat her to it and opened it to find Remy Montagne, Maurice's boss and the leader of the Bayou Brotherhood Protectors. And he was holding a pizza box. "Anyone hungry?"

The scent of warm pizza, tomato sauce and cheese filled the air, making Amelie's stomach rumble loudly. She pressed a hand to her belly, heat rising into her cheeks.

Maurice grinned. "Lunch was enough, was it?"

"It was until I smelled pizza." She hurried over. "Tell me it has pepperoni on it."

Remy laughed. "It has everything on it. Except anchovies. Shelby thought you might need sustenance, and I thought I'd get a sitrep on what's going on."

"Is Shelby on duty?" Amelie asked.

"On baby duty," Remy clarified. "She sent me out on the pizza run. I can't stay long. I have another pizza in the truck. But I wanted to get the details of what happened last night straight from the horses' mouths. I also had a call from Hank Patterson, asking if we needed any further assistance other than Swede's technical support."

"Come into the front of the shop where we can set the pizza down on one of the bistro tables." Amelie led the way through the kitchen into the front of the bakery, switching on lights along the way.

While Remy dropped the pizza box on a table, Maurice filled him in on what had occurred the night before.

Amelie turned on the coffee maker, measured coffee into the filter and poured in water.

She found paper plates and napkins they'd just stocked on a shelf behind the counter and brought them to the table.

"Which brings us to our trip to New Orleans." Maurice opened the box and let Amelie select a slice first.

"What happened in New Orleans that made you get Swede working on researching a French family and a German dude?" Remy asked.

Amelie gave him a brief rundown of her work in Paris, her mentor, Armand, and Luis, the chef's son. Then she told him about getting a call from Luis and their subsequent lunch meeting.

"Sounds like Schulz was looking for lost or stolen art or antiquities," Remy said. "Which is a little odd, considering the Nazi's stole so much artwork, and some of it disappeared."

"I thought the same," Maurice said.

"I spent a lot of time with Armand over the four years I worked with him," Amelie said. "I never once saw any artwork or antiquities in his flat in Paris or in his restaurant. And he never mentioned owning any. As far as I could tell from the stories he shared about his parents' escape from Paris and subsequent return, they had very little and had to start over. You'd think that if they'd managed to get artwork out of Paris, they might've sold it at some point."

"Maybe they did." Remy's brow wrinkled. "Schulz might be tracing back through their journey to find who they sold it to."

"That could be a challenge," Maurice said, "without knowing what the artwork or antiques were, and the people who sold and bought the item or items aren't around to ask."

"That's why we're lucky having access to a computer genius like Swede," Remy said with a grin. "If there's information out there, he'll find it. I suspect there are some records, especially if Schulz knew enough to chase down Armand Benoît's son to see if he knew anything about family treasures."

A chill slithered down the back of Amelie's neck. "Do you think the break-in here at my bakery had anything to do with whatever it is Fredrick Schulz is looking for?"

Remy frowned. "Good question."

Maurice's eyes narrowed. "You did spend more time with Armand Benoît than his own son. If Schulz was able to find Luis in California, he could've stumbled across the fact you were close to Armand—"

"—and came to Bayou Mambaloa to search my bakery?" Amelie shook her head. It sounded too bizarre.

"You said yourself, nothing was missing," Remy reminded her.

"But the vandal destroyed so much. If he was looking for a painting or an antique, why rip everything apart?"

"Unless the item is small…like a pocket watch?" Maurice offered.

Amelie's heart skipped a beat. "Do you think whoever broke into my bakery might go after Luis because of the pocket watch?"

"I sent the photos I took of the watch to Swede and asked him to see if it was worth anything," Maurice said. "I also asked him if he could figure out what the numbers mean."

"Show me the photos," Remy said.

Maurice pulled out his phone, brought up the pictures and handed the phone to his boss.

After studying the images, Remy shook his head. "No idea. Maybe it's a combination or code for something."

"I'd think it's too many numbers for a combination lock," Maurice said.

"The number of a bank account?" Remy guessed.

Maurice's brow dipped. "Maybe. Some European bank account numbers are really long."

Remy nodded. "If it is a bank account, Swede will figure it out." He glanced from Maurice to Amelie. "Any other revelations I should be aware of?"

Amelie met Maurice's gaze. They shook their heads in unison.

Maurice's mouth quirked at the corners.

That slight upward movement sent warmth

flowing through Amelie as if they'd shared a moment. Which was ridiculous.

She turned her attention back to Remy. "I take it the sheriff's department hasn't come up with a suspect for the break-in."

Remy's lips pressed together. "No. I'm sorry. The latent prints were mostly yours, and there were too many in the front from customers. They suspect that whoever broke in was wearing gloves."

Maurice snorted. "They should look for a suspect with flour all over those gloves and his shoes."

"I'll be sure to remind Shelby, although I'm sure she already knows." He smiled. "In the meantime, enjoy your pizza. I need to get mine home. I'm sure Shelby's getting hangry by now. And I have bath duty tonight, which means Jean-Luc and I will both be soaked. That little guy loves playing in the water."

Maurice and Amelie walked Remy to the back door and let him out, locking the door behind him.

They returned to the pizza, ate quickly and got back to work.

Amelie put Maurice to work measuring flour and buttering bread pans, while she mixed dough, kneaded and shaped it, then set the bread to rise.

Once she had the bread dough where she wanted it, she worked on preparing pastries and then cookies. By the time nine o'clock rolled around, Amelie was sagging against the counter, her feet, back and head ached, but she was ready for the next day. Her baked goods were ready, her kitchen was clean and she'd only missed one day of sales.

She smiled. "Wow." She hung her apron on a hook on the wall and turned her smile on Maurice. "We did it. Now, all I have to do is put things in the oven tomorrow morning. Baked with Love will be open as usual tomorrow morning." Tired beyond measure, tears welled in her eyes. "I couldn't have done it without you."

Maurice pulled her into his arms. "I have no doubt you would've done just fine without me, but thanks."

She laid her cheek on his shoulder and wrapped her arms around his waist. "If you ever want a job as a sous chef, I'd hire you in a heartbeat."

He chuckled, his arms tightening around her. "Be careful. I might take you up on the offer." He rested his chin on top of her hair.

"I meant it. It's been a while since I've had help in the kitchen. Actually, since New Orleans almost two years ago."

"I'm glad I wasn't in your way. You were amazing. You didn't let a little setback knock you for a loop." He tipped her head back.

She blinked back the tears filling her eyes.

Maurice frowned. "Hey, why the tears?"

"I don't know," she said and sniffed. "Tired, I guess. It's the first time we've slowed down since the break-in."

"Let's lock up and get you upstairs. You need that sleep." He leaned forward and pressed his lips to her forehead.

Amelie's pulse quickened, pushing exhaustion to the back of her mind and a different need overpowered her desire for sleep.

Maybe it was delirium from lack of sleep, or relief that she'd managed to pull off a miracle. Whatever it was made Amelie lean up on her toes and press her lips to his.

As soon as her mouth connected with his, heat flowed through her chest, into her arms and legs and coiled low in her belly. Her hands slid up his chest to lace behind his neck, bringing him closer.

She opened to him.

For a second, he hesitated.

Had she made a mistake? Was she pushing for something he wasn't feeling?

Then he claimed her mouth, swept her tongue

with his in a sensuous dance, crushing her to his chest.

What had started as a kiss to her forehead ended in a fiery connection that shook her world.

When at last he loosened his hold, she drew in a shaky breath, her hands sliding down to his chest. "I'm sorry," she murmured.

"For what?" Maurice brushed a strand of her hair that had escaped the net cap back behind her ear.

"I shouldn't have...kissed you." Suddenly embarrassed, she refused to meet his gaze. "I'd better go to bed before I do something else you might regret."

He tipped her chin upward until she was forced to look him in the eyes. "I think there were two sides to that kiss, in case you didn't notice."

"Yeah, but you hesitated," she shook her head. "You didn't have to kiss me back."

"But I did." He touched his lips to the tip of her nose and set her at arm's length. "Look, we're both tired to the point we're half-drunk. We both need sleep. Let's get you up to your apartment and sort through all this tomorrow, after we've slept and our heads are clear."

Amelie wrapped her arms around herself and nodded. "You're right. I don't know what came over me. I need sleep." She turned and hurried toward the back door.

Maurice beat her to it and stepped outside first. Once he'd had a chance to look around, he opened the door wider and held it for her.

Amelie exited, turned and locked the bakery with the new key. When she turned to go up to her apartment, Maurice was at her side. "You don't have to—"

"Yes, I do. I'm here to protect you. Until they find the vandal, you're not safe."

"I have a new lock and key."

"What if he's good at picking locks? After I clear the apartment, you can kick me out." He walked up the stairs beside her and held out his hand for the key.

Amelie dug it out of her pocket and laid it in his hand. Touching his palm sent fire racing through her once again. She fought the urge to fling herself into his arms and beg him to kiss her again.

Maurice's face showed nothing of what he might be thinking. No sign that he wanted to kiss her again. No sign of anything.

He unlocked the door and stepped inside. Less than a minute later, he was back. "All clear."

Amelie entered her apartment. It looked the same as it had after they'd cleaned up the mess earlier that day. Had it been just that morning? It felt more like a lifetime since she'd entered her apartment last.

"Lock the door behind me," Maurice said behind her.

She spun to see him standing on the landing, pulling the door closed between them.

Amelie, suddenly afraid, put out a hand to stop him. "Are you leaving me?"

He shook his head. "I'll sleep out here."

She shook her head. "You can't sleep out there. What if it rains?"

"The chance of rain tonight is less than ten percent."

"But you can't sleep out there."

"I'm not leaving," he said.

"Then come inside and sleep on the sofa."

He shook his head.

"Please," she whispered. "I promise not to throw myself at you again."

His lips twitched. "I'm not afraid of that."

She frowned. "Then what are you afraid of?"

"I'm afraid I might not be able to control myself with you."

Her heartbeat fluttered and then raced. "What if I'm okay with that?"

He sighed and stepped through the door and

stood in front of her without reaching out to hold her. "Amelie, you're a beautiful, amazing woman. The kind of woman who deserves a man who can commit to her."

Amelie nodded. "And you're not the kind of man who wants to commit."

Maurice shook his head. "I don't know if I can."

Again, Amelie nodded. "I understand."

"Do you?"

"I think so." She lifted her chin. "But I refuse to let you sleep out on the landing. You'll sleep on the sofa. If it makes you feel better, I'll lock my bedroom door—and I won't try to kiss you again." She stuck out her hand. "Deal?"

He stared down at her hand for a moment and then back up into her eyes. "I'm sorry."

"Don't be. I was tired and a little loopy." She forced a smile. "Forget about it. We'll just be friends." She kept her hand out.

Eventually, he took it, gave it a gentle shake and let go too quickly.

"You can shower first." She reached around him, closed the door and turned the deadbolt. "I'm going to pour a glass of wine."

Maurice showered in record time, emerging from her bedroom before Amelie was halfway through her glass of wine. He came out wearing his jeans and nothing else, a towel wrapped around his naked shoulders.

She held up her glass. "Want one?"

"I do."

"You can help yourself to anything in the fridge." Amelie forced herself to walk calmly into her room, resisting the urge to dive through and slam the door behind her.

Once inside, she closed the door softly and slid to the floor, careful not to spill her wine. The tears she'd held at bay slid down her cheeks. She swallowed hard to keep a sob from rising up her throat.

"What's wrong with me?" she whispered.

"Did you say something?" Maurice's voice sounded through the door.

"No," she choked out. "I'm fine." Just fine.

Then why did she feel like she was falling apart?

One kiss shouldn't have left her an emotional wreck.

She tipped back her wine glass, swallowing the last of the liquid and letting it numb her heart. Then she did what she always did. She picked herself up by the bootstraps and got on with life.

Though, knowing Maurice was on the other side of the door, half-naked and completely immune to her...

Or was he?

Either way, she'd offered him sex with no strings attached.

And he'd refused.

Well, that sucked lemons.

CHAPTER 6

Maurice stared up at the ceiling in Amelie's apartment, his head resting on one arm of the sofa, his legs draped over the other end. He debated stretching out on the floor, but doubted he'd be any more comfortable there.

He wouldn't be comfortable anywhere at the moment when all he could think about was the clear invitation Amelie had offered for him to have uncommitted, no strings attached sex with her.

No matter how tired he was, his head swam with all the possibilities, all the reasons he could use to convince himself it was all right.

Uncommitted sex.

What was wrong with that? They were both consenting adults.

Stupid. Stupid. Stupid.

Maurice sat up and was halfway off the sofa when logic overrode baser instincts.

What he'd told her was the truth. He hadn't taken their relationship further because she deserved better. Amelie deserved someone who could commit to something more than a one-night stand. Someone who would be there for her, always.

Someone who could save her when the shit hit the fan.

When his memories replayed the horror of the mission that had ended with the death of his fiancée, he swore he could still smell the chemical, garlic scent of phosphorous and feel the pain of it eating away at his own hand. He could almost feel the pain Sandy had felt with the chemical burning into the back of her skull.

They'd gone in to rescue two soldiers. Both men had lived.

Yet Maurice had failed to save the one he'd loved enough to ask her to marry him.

He couldn't commit to another woman after that. What if he promised to love, honor and protect someone like Amelie? Would he fail to fulfill his promise? Could he survive losing her when he did?

The hardest part of going through rehab hadn't

been learning how to be proficient with his left hand. Working with the psychologist had been the most painful. He hated that all he'd lost was the partial use of his dominant hand. Sandy had lost her life. Why had he lived and she'd died? No amount of counseling could answer that question in his mind. For the past few years, he'd trudged through life, survivor's guilt weighing him down so heavily he was an emotional zombie. Yes, he considered himself part of the team and pulled his weight. He did a good job on each assignment. But he was in an emotional wasteland, unable to pull himself out.

When he'd seen Amelie frowning on the edge of the dance floor at the Crawdad Hole, the protector in him had rallied and stepped up. Perhaps he'd sensed someone hurting from a similar loss. Or not.

Whatever it was, he'd been drawn to Amelie more than any other woman since Sandy.

Being with her when she'd discovered her life's work in shambles had been eye-opening. She'd only allowed herself a few minutes of despair before she'd pulled herself together and gone right back to work.

She was strong and independent.

Amelie's determination and can-do attitude

had breathed new light and optimism into Maurice.

Working side by side with her over the long day had been the kick in the pants he'd needed to get on with his own life.

Then why had he backed off when she'd offered herself to him?

He sank back onto the sofa and closed his eyes. Perhaps, if he slept on it, he might have all the answers. As tired as he was, he sure as hell wasn't coming up with any.

HE MUST HAVE FALLEN asleep sometime after midnight.

The sound of a door opening woke him in the dark hours of the morning. He leaped to his feet and assumed a ready stance, his gaze going to the door of her apartment.

"I'm sorry," a soft voice said behind him. "I didn't mean to wake you."

Maurice spun to face a fully dressed Amelie, silhouetted by the soft light coming from behind her. She'd pulled her dark hair back in a ponytail and wore jeans and a pastel pink T-shirt.

Maurice scrubbed a hand down his face, even

more exhausted than when he'd lain down on the couch. "What time is it?"

"Three-thirty," she responded and walked through the room without turning on a light. "I have to get the ovens going."

"I'll help," he said.

"You should stay and sleep longer. I do this by myself all the time."

"You haven't had a break-in until the night before last," he reminded her. "Give me a minute to get my shoes on. I'm coming with you."

She nodded, went to her refrigerator in the corner of the kitchenette and pulled out a small tub of yogurt. "Can I interest you in yogurt?"

"No, thank you. I know it's supposed to be good for you and all, but I never learned to like it." He bent to pull his boots on one at a time, then stood. Maurice grabbed his T-shirt from where he'd dropped it on the end table and pulled it over his head. Less than awake, but determined to escort Amelie downstairs, Maurice walked toward the door and paused with his hand on the doorknob. "Now, when you get those eclairs baked, I'd be more than happy to take one off your hands. Ready?"

She walked up behind him. "Deal. And yes, I'm ready."

He opened the door, stepped out onto the landing and glanced around at the dark shadows surrounding the building. Nothing moved. Before the butt-crack of dawn, who would be stupid enough to be out and about?

A baker on her way to get ready to open her doors for the early risers on their way to work—that's who.

Once again, he had to admire her drive and determination to make her business a success. As she stepped out onto the landing, she turned to him with a smile. "One éclair seems a small price to pay for all your help." She glanced up at him, her eyebrows rising. "Did you sleep well last night?"

He sure the hell hadn't, but he wasn't going to admit to it. "Yeah."

She held his gaze a little longer, her lips curving. "Good. I worried you wouldn't be comfortable." She turned and started down the stairs, adding as if an afterthought, "…on the sofa."

The sofa had been only a fraction of the problem leading to his sleep-inhibited night. Thoughts of making love to Amelie, possibly lying naked in the bed on the other side of her door, a few short feet away, had kept him awake. Add to that his survivor's guilt and internal battle over whether he should or shouldn't make a move on someone after his failure to protect his fiancée had led to her death. Yeah, his sleep had been doomed before he'd even closed his eyes.

As soon as they entered the bakery kitchen, Amelie made a beeline for the coffeemaker and started a fresh batch of fragrant brew.

Maurice thanked the gods for coffee. He stood close to the pot and inhaled the aroma as the magic elixir brewed.

Amelie went to work preheating ovens and pulling dough out of refrigerators. Soon, the kitchen was filled with the scent of coffee and baking bread.

"What can I do to help?" he asked her.

"Stack cookies in the display case." She showed him what to do, handed him a pair of rubber gloves, a tray of cookies she'd baked the night before, and set him to work.

In the cabinet, Maurice arranged chocolate-chip and oatmeal-raisin cookies. Alongside those, he lined up pralines and peanut brittle.

In between batches, he sipped on the best coffee he'd ever tasted, the caffeine reviving him.

Maurice was wide awake by the time the bakery opened bright and early at six o'clock.

Customers streamed in for their morning cup of coffee or a shot of espresso and one of Amelie's pastries that melted in their mouths as soon as it touched their tongues.

Maurice had known the draw well before he'd gotten to know the woman behind the magic. Now, he loved the pastries even more.

Amelie had a gift she chose to share with the people of Bayou Mambaloa, and they were grateful, expressing their gratitude in moans of delight.

After the first rush of the morning, Amelie came to stand beside Maurice, a fresh cup of coffee in her hands. "Are you surviving?" she asked.

He nodded. "We're practically sold out of eclairs. Do you have more in the oven?"

Amelie nodded. "They'll be out in five minutes."

"Everyone who has come in this morning expressed their concern over yesterday's closure." Maurice gave a crooked smile. "Apparently, news travels fast in the community."

Amelie nodded and sighed. "It does. I imagine the news about the break-in went out even before law enforcement arrived."

Maurice's lips twisted. "It's hard to believe the sheriff's department hasn't found a single suspect."

Amelie leaned against the display case, her gaze on the window overlooking Main Street. "Apparently, whoever broke into my shop and apartment had the foresight to wear gloves, thus hampering law enforcement's investigations into their nefarious activities." She shook her head. "What would the vandal be looking for in my bakery?"

"Great eclairs?"

"He didn't take any of the baked goods," Amelie said.

"Hopefully, Swede will come up with something soon." Maurice straightened the row of chocolate chip cookies. "In the meantime, how about taking a break? You've been on your feet for hours."

"I could do that." Amelie sank onto a chair at one of the bistro tables and took a sip of her coffee.

Maurice poured another cup and joined her.

As soon as he sat, the chirping of a cell phone sounded behind the counter.

When Amelie started to rise, Maurice held up a hand. "I'll get it." He retrieved her cell phone and brought it to her.

"It's a text from Luis." Amelie glanced down at the text. "He says he's sorry he got busy last night and forgot to take pictures of the photographs he'd kept. He just sent them." Amelie brought up the first black-and-white photo of Armand's young parents, standing in front of the St. Louis Cathedral in New Orleans.

Maurice recognized the location, having been there a number of times.

Armand's mother had her arm hooked through his father's. She was smiling. He stood with his shoulders back, his expression unreadable, holding a pocket watch in his hand.

"Is that—" Amelie pointed at the photo.

"The watch Luis showed us?" Maurice pulled out his cell phone and brought up the images he'd taken when they'd been with Luis. "It's the same one."

"So, we know Armand's father had the watch when he lived in New Orleans and have proof it belonged to him." Amelie shrugged. "What does it mean?"

"Maybe nothing," Maurice said. "Or something. We don't have enough information to even speculate."

Amelie flipped the screen to the next photo.

Armand's parents posed in the living room of what once must have been their estate, before the German occupation. His father sat in a wingback chair, wearing a dark business suit. His mother stood beside him, wearing a classy skirt suit with broad shoulders, the waistline cinched in with a wide matching belt.

Maurice studied the room in the background.

A fancy white mantel surrounded a wood-burning fireplace. On either side of the mantel were what appeared to be porcelain plates on stands with a small bouquet of flowers between them.

Over the mantel was a painting of a stream or river with a path alongside it. On the path was a woman, carrying a parasol. Maurice couldn't tell for sure, but it seemed to be an impressionistic painting.

"Could that be a Monet?" Amelie asked, her tone low, intense.

"It's hard to tell in a black and white photo," Maurice said. "Maybe. Send them to me, and I'll forward them to Swede."

Moments later, Maurice had the images and texted them to Swede with the message that they were of Armand's parents, some of them before WWII, and the one taken in New Orleans with the watch in his hand.

A woman entered the bakery, calling a halt to Amelie's break. She rose with a smile and called out a greeting, slipping quickly behind the counter to take the lady's order.

Maurice collected their coffee cups and carried them into the kitchen, poured the cold coffee into the sink and placed the cups into the dishwasher.

When he went back out to the front, the woman had finished her purchase and was walking out the door.

A middle-aged blond-haired man in neatly pressed slacks, a polo shirt and a blazer held the door for the woman until she passed through, then entered.

The man approached the counter with a smile. "I am looking for Ms. Amelie Aubert," he said with a hint of a German accent.

Maurice tensed and moved closer to Amelie.

The smile of greeting Amelie wore slipped. "That's me. How can I help you?"

The man held out his hand. "I'm Fredrick Schulz. I am currently researching the flight of wealthy French families who left France during WWII. I understand you worked with Armand Benoît in Paris a few years ago."

Amelie nodded. "I did."

"His parents, Germaine and Celine Benoît, were just such a family able to escape before Nazi occupation. I had hoped to learn more about them through journals, diaries or stories passed down to their son, Armand. Unfortunately, Armand is deceased, and his son, Luis, had little knowledge of his father's family, having lived with his mother in California for most of his life."

"What do you want from me?" Amelie asked.

"Did Armand Benoît speak to you of his parents' journey? Where they went and how they survived in exile?"

Maurice's brow dipped. "Even if she knew anything, why should she tell you? Why is it important for you to know more about the Benoîts?"

Schulz lifted his chin. "I am a historian of the arts. I am also German. As a German, I understand many famous paintings and antiquities were stolen, hidden or lost during WWII by Nazis and their sympathizers. I am trying to determine whether the Benoîts were able to escape with their prized art and antiquities or if they left them in their home for the Nazis to steal. I have been studying letters and records from the team Hitler assembled to identify artworks from wealthy collectors, which they targeted for works to be added to the *Führermuseum* in Linz. The Benoîts were among the names listed, with a note that they had defected. No other historical accounts indicate whether they escaped with their collection or if the works were confiscated by the regime. Did Armand have any artwork that you knew of?"

"Armand Benoît was first and foremost a master chef. He lived and breathed his work.

Outside the Chez Benoît, his life was minimalistic. Small flat, limited furniture and little decoration." Amelie lifted her chin, her jaw tight. "Upon his death, everything he owned was donated to the poor. His son was heading back to California and didn't want any of the furnishings. There was no artwork. I don't know what else to tell you."

"Did he say whether or not his parents passed artwork to him that he might have sold before you met him?" Schulz asked.

Amelie shook her head. "No."

"Did Mr. Benoît tell you that his parents came to New Orleans?"

Amelie hesitated and then answered, "He did mention it."

"Did he say how they supported themselves?"

"His mother worked in a bakery, his father in a shipyard."

"Did he say whether or not they sold any valuables to help them through that time or to fund their return trip?"

Amelie looked as though she was starting to get irritated with the German's direct questioning. The man didn't exude a hint of charm, just cold manners. "What I've told you already is everything Armand told me of his parents' time in New Orleans."

"Did he say anything about their return? Did they sell any valuables upon their return?" Schulz asked.

"He said nothing about them selling valuables," Amelie said. "They worked hard to rebuild their lives."

Gisele Gautier, owner of the Mamba Wamba Art and Gifts shop, entered the bakery in one of her colorful, flowing skirts, her dark, curly hair hanging in waves down to her waist. With her mocha-colored skin, warm like sunlit earth, and golden eyes, she stood with her arms crossed over her chest, exuding the confidence of a voodoo queen like her infamous grandmother. The air practically crackled around her.

Maurice smiled, knowing his buddy, Rafael, had his hands full with the petite powerhouse.

Amelie caught sight of her friend and seemed to gather strength from her. Her back straightened, and her chin rose. "Mr. Schulz, that's all I know," she said with a tight smile. "Now, if you'll excuse me, I have a business to run."

Schulz wasn't done. "Ms. Aubert, unlike my countrymen who stole art, I wish to protect it and see that others can view and appreciate works of great masters." He pulled a business card out of his blazer pocket and handed it to her. "If you remember anything else, please contact me. Others might not be as willing to share great works with all of humanity. Thank you for your time." He gave Maurice a curt nod, performed an about-face and left the bakery.

Gisele waited until the door closed behind the man before she cocked an eyebrow in Amelie and Maurice's direction. "Did I detect a foreign accent?"

Amelie let go of a long, slow breath and read the name on the business card. "Yes. Fredrick Schulz. European Art Historian, based out of Frankfurt, Germany."

Gisele's brow wrinkled. "What's he doing in Bayou Mambaloa?"

"He wanted information about my former mentor and friend, Armand Benoît."

"What's an art historian want with a Parisian chef?" Gisele rounded the counter and hugged Amelie. "And why didn't you call me to come help you clean up after the break-in?"

Amelie held her friend for a long moment before glancing up to meet Maurice's gaze. "I had all the support I needed."

Gisele stepped back, glancing toward Maurice. "Shelby told me you'd taken on the assignment to protect our girl, Amelie. She didn't say you'd be helping her run the bakery." Her gaze switched to Amelie. "I'm sure he's been more than helpful. Rafael's team has been the best thing to happen to Bayou Mambaloa." Her brow dipped before she turned back to Maurice. "You'd better do right by our sweet baker, you hear?"

"Or what? You'll put a voodoo spell on him?" Amelie laughed.

Gisele's eyes narrowed. "I might. There are perks to being the granddaughter of Bayou Mambaloa's voodoo queen."

Maurice held up his hands. "I'll do my best."

Gisele nodded. "And don't go breakin' her heart. If she leaves town because you hurt her, I won't have to put a spell on you. The community will feed you to the alligators."

Maurice didn't know whether to laugh or be afraid. The petite granddaughter of the voodoo queen was known to be a formidable opponent. And her grandmother...? Well, no one crossed her. "I'm here to protect Amelie, not break her heart or anyone else's."

"*Mon cher*, let's see what da spirits got waitin' for you two." Gisele took one of Amelie's hands and one of Maurice's, closed her eyes and tipped her head back. For a long moment, she said nothing, her face relaxing, her body swaying slightly.

Maurice wanted to laugh at Gisele's theatrics, but the room went so still he couldn't push air through his lungs. It was as if time stood still and froze him to the spot.

Gisele's eyelids twitched, and a soft moan rose from her throat. In a low voice barely above a whisper, her Cajun accent more pronounced, she half-spoke, half-sang.

"SPIRITS BE STIRRIN',
Dark waters will rise.
Dance once with death
To reach the far side.
Through the dark night,
Let hope be your guide.
Trust your heart, cher—
For love will survive."

A COOL WAFT of air blew across Maurice, raising gooseflesh on his arms. He tried to pull his hand free of Gisele's, but her grip tightened around his, holding him in place a second longer.

His gaze met Amelie's across Gisele's petite form.

Amelie's eyes were wide and a little glassy. A shiver shook her frame.

Gisele straightened, dropped their hands and blinked. "I guess the spirits weren't communing." She shrugged. "Whatever. You two will figure it out together. I have to get back to the gift shop before Johnny starts cursing at customers."

Amelie gave a shaky laugh. "I'm surprised you let that parrot stay in the shop. Doesn't he offend your customers?"

Gisele chuckled. "Absolutely. I think that's why they come back. Now, I came for a loaf of your bread, if you've had time to make some. Rafael asked for a club sandwich for lunch."

"I have some." Amelie rubbed her arms as she moved toward the bread wrapped in cellophane. She handed it to Gisele and stared at the woman. "You know you gave us a prediction, don't you?"

Gisele's eyebrows rose. "Did I?"

Amelie and Maurice nodded as one.

"Hmm," Gisele said with a satisfied nod. "If you say I did, I guess I did." She tucked the loaf of bread under her arm and handed Amelie a bill to pay.

Amelie pushed the money back at Gisele. "Consider it a peace-offering to the spirit. A request to go easy on us."

Gisele pursed her lips. "Must've been a doozy of a message."

"You don't remember any of it?" Maurice remembered every word as if it had been seared into his brain.

"Not a word." Her brow wrinkled. "Was it bad?"

Amelie rubbed her arms again. "It could be."

"Definitely creepy," Maurice added.

"I'm sure that, together, you will come through." Gisele patted Amelie's arm. "Be safe, my friend." With the bread tucked under her arm, she floated out of the bakery, singing something that sounded like abracadabra.

Amelie's gaze followed her friend out the door. "What do you suppose her words meant?" She turned to Maurice.

"I don't know," he said.

"Do you remember what she said?"

He nodded and repeated Gisele's prediction, word for word,

"Spirits be stirrin',

Dark waters will rise.

Dance once with death

To reach the far side.

Through the dark night,

Let hope be your guide.

Trust your heart, cher—
For love will survive."

Amelie shook her head, her brow creased. "What spirits?"

His eyebrow rose. "You believe all that Voodoo mumbo jumbo?"

"Whether you believe it or not, being forewarned means we can be forearmed. Think." Amelie paced behind the counter. *"Spirits be stirrin'.* Like ghosts?"

When Maurice didn't respond, Amelie glared at him. "Seriously. I've seen results from some of Gisele's predictions, potions and spells."

Maurice sighed and chose to participate in the riddle, even if he wasn't convinced Voodoo was real. "Spirits could be the ghosts of the past."

Her eyes met his. "Armand, Germaine and Celine Benoît? Or Nazis?"

"Let's go with Germaine and Celine Benoît. They had a lot to lose, leaving their home in Paris."

"Dark waters will rise." Amelie chewed on her bottom lip, drawing Maurice's attention to it, and making him want to kiss it.

He dragged his thoughts back to the riddle.

"The bayou is full of dark water. It could rise in a storm."

"Okay, sounds good," Amelie said, nodding. "How about *dance once with death?*"

A heaviness settled in Maurice's chest. He hadn't liked this part of the prediction. He'd danced with death and lost his fiancée in the process. "Could it be someone will try to kill one of us?" Maurice asked, though he hated even saying the words. If one of them was targeted, he prayed it would be him, not Amelie. Or that he'd be able to save her this time.

"Or both?" Amelie suggested. "I know you'll have my back. I'll have yours as well."

Maurice smiled at the image that rose in his mind of Amelie, a Valkyrie with her sword held high to protect her man.

Only he wasn't her man.

That thought made his smile slip. She deserved a man worthy of her devotion. That wasn't him.

"We'll have to keep our eyes open for danger," she said and touched his arm. "I'm glad I have you for protection."

He hoped he lived up to her expectations. *"Through the dark night, let hope be your guide.* Whatever happens could be at night."

"Maybe…" Amelie tilted her head. "Or it could

be evil casting a dark pall on us, versus the literal darkness of night."

Maurice nodded. "So, we can't bank on danger occurring at night."

"Trust your heart, cher—For love will survive," Amelie said softly. "Whose love? The ghosts'? Armand's love for his estranged wife? His love for his son?"

Maurice didn't say it, but the thought sprang to his mind. *Amelie.*

Amelie would survive.

Another thought followed on the heels of that one. Would he fall in love with her? Would she fall in love with him?

Maurice reminded himself that the prediction was a bunch of voodoo nonsense. He wasn't going to fall in love with Amelie. She wasn't going to fall in love with him. Gisele didn't have to worry that he would break Amelie's heart.

Amelie scrubbed her hands down her face. "Between Mr. Schulz's visit and Gisele's ominous prophecy, I'm a little..." She wrapped her arms around her middle and shook her head.

"Freaked out? Unnerved? Disturbed?"

Her lips twitched and spread into a smile. "Hungry."

Maurice barked out a laugh, the tension leaving the air. "What time do you close?"

She glanced at the clock on the wall. "In an hour."

"What say you and I get some dinner at Tante Mimi's diner?"

She nodded. "I have to prepare tomorrow's dough and pastries before I leave. Fortunately, the shop is closed. What I cook in the morning is for delivery to Broussard's Country Store. They sell my baked goods on Monday so that I can have the day off. I can get started on tomorrow's pastries. I can start that in between customers."

Maurice glanced toward the front. "I can handle anyone coming in. Go. Do your thing. Just keep that back door locked."

Rather than leave it up to chance, he followed her into the kitchen in the back and twisted the deadbolt, locking the back door to keep anyone from wandering in who didn't belong.

He touched her cheek, loving that she was just as beautiful with her hair in a net as she was with it down. Though he could easily imagine it spread out across a pillowcase, her breasts bare, her hazel eyes dark with passion.

His cell phone chirped with an incoming text.

As he stood between the front of the shop and the kitchen, he glanced down at the text.

"It's Swede. He says he's identified the painting hanging over the mantel in the Benoît home." He looked up and met Amelie's gaze. "It's one of the paintings considered lost during WWII." He paused. "It's a Monet."

CHAPTER 7

AMELIE SAT across the table from Maurice in Tante Mimi's diner. She'd barely touched the burger and fries she'd ordered. Hell, she never ordered a burger because of the caloric intake she allotted herself. What had she been thinking?

That was just it. She hadn't been able to think once Maurice had given her the news from Swede.

"A Monet?" she whispered for the tenth time, glancing around as if the diner might be full of spies. "The Benoîts owned a Monet?"

"Swede matched it with a color photo that dated back to 1939 and the record of the sale of a relatively unknown painting titled *Lady by the Stream* by Impressionist artist Claude Monet from a private art collector to Germaine Benoît for one-hundred-fifty-thousand Francs."

"That has to be what Schulz is looking for," Amelie said. "How could something that unique and precious just disappear?"

"Armand told you his parents packed up their belongings and valuables and left their estate."

"He did," Amelie agreed.

"They had to have taken it with them."

Amelie nodded. "They hid in the country until they could get on a boat to the US."

"They could've hidden the painting in the place where they were lying low in France," Maurice said. "Armand didn't mention where they hid, did he?"

"No. I'm not sure he knew. He was pretty good at remembering details. If his parents had told him where they'd hidden, he would've remembered."

"And he didn't mention what they took with them on the ship to the US? I wonder if there are copies of the ship manifests from that timeframe. If we could find the ship they were on, it might tell us something about how much luggage the Benoîts brought with them."

"Finding a manifest from the ship the Benoîts were on would be like finding a needle in a haystack."

Maurice's lips curled.

Amelie's curved as well. "Let me guess. Swede is good at finding needles in haystacks?"

"He is." Maurice grinned. "What month did you say the Benoîts left Paris?"

"Early June."

Maurice keyed information into his cell phone and sent a text to Swede. "He might find records of the ships that left France headed for the United States around that time."

"Would they have used their own names to book passage?"

"Maybe," Maurice said. "It doesn't hurt to search on their names."

The door to the diner swung open.

Amelie frowned as Fredrick Schulz entered. The man's forehead creased in a frown as he scanned the room. When his gaze landed on Amelie and Maurice, he spun and marched toward them.

"Incoming," Maurice murmured.

Amelie tensed. "I see him."

Maurice rose from his chair and blocked the man from getting to Amelie. He tipped his head back and stared down his nose at the German, five inches shorter than Maurice. "Ms. Aubert has already told you everything she knew from her conversations with her former employer, Armand Benoît."

"I have information she might want to hear."

Amelie touched Maurice's back. "Let him talk," she said.

Maurice didn't move for a good thirty seconds, staring down at the smaller man. "Hurt her, and you might not live to regret it," he said in a low, resonant tone.

Schulz raised his hands. "I did not come here to hurt anyone. I am here to keep her from getting hurt."

"It's okay," Amelie assured Maurice. "I want to hear what he has to say."

Maurice glared at the smaller man before he stepped aside. He remained within reach to move swiftly if he needed to dive in to break up a fight or keep Schulz from hurting Amelie.

Schulz slid into the booth opposite Amelie.

Maurice sat next to Amelie and leaned forward enough that, if he had to, he could fling his body across hers to keep her safe.

"Ms. Aubert," Schulz started, "I fear you are in grave danger."

"The dark waters," Amelie murmured low enough that Fredrick couldn't make out her words.

The brief narrowing of Maurice's eyes indicated he'd caught her words and meaning.

"How am I in danger?" Amelie asked. "I don't know anything about the Benoîts other than what Armand told me."

"From the letters and records acquired from WWII," the German said, "we know the Benoîts owned a very beautiful and priceless painting by Claude Monet."

Irritation, bordering on anger, flashed through Amelie.

So, Schulz had known about the specific painting that Amelie and Maurice had only just learned about.

"Why didn't you tell us about the painting when you came to my bakery?" Amelie frowned. "And from Luis's account, you didn't mention it when you visited him in California."

"Please accept my apologies for not being more transparent. I wished to gauge how much you knew. From both your reaction and that of Armand's son, Luis, I realized you had no knowledge of the painting's existence."

"Did you reveal to Armand the specific painting you were researching?" Maurice asked.

The German shook his head. "No."

"How does a Monet painting that disappeared

during WWII place me in danger?" Amelie asked. "I didn't even know it existed until today."

"Perhaps, I should explain my obsession with the painting."

"We're listening," Maurice said, his tone tense.

Schulz dipped his head. "I have spent many hours, days, years in the U.S. National Archives and Records Administration, looking through the photo albums and records listing almost every piece of art either sold or identified as being in France prior to the occupation. Over three years ago, I came across the Monet owned by Germaine Benoît. It was marked with the status of 'lost.' Something about the woman in the painting captivated me. She has haunted me ever since." He drew in a breath and let it out slowly. "I immediately flew to Paris to interview Germaine's only descendant, Armand Benoît, hoping to discover the painting's whereabouts. After our meeting, I knew I would have to trace his parents' journey if I had any hope of finding the *Lady by the Stream*."

"And?" Amelie prompted impatiently.

"I have followed leads for missing artwork for decades. In the last four or five years, some of the works I've located have been stolen before I could get to them first." He shook his head. "If you look up my record, you will see that I have never kept one of my findings. I meet with the former owners and/or their descendants to determine the appropriate disposition. I was deeply concerned over the thefts and afraid I was leading the thieves to those priceless items."

"What does that have to do with me?"

"You and Armand Benoît's son were the last known people to have contact with him before he was found dead in his restaurant." Schulz leaned closer.

Maurice semi-blocked Amelie's body with his without saying anything.

"I spoke to Armand two days before he died," Schulz blurted.

Amelie touched a hand to her chest, an image of Armand lying on the floor of his beloved kitchen filling her thoughts. She swallowed hard to force the lump rising in her throat back down.

The German continued. "He told me much the same story as you have relayed."

"You spoke to Armand?" Amelie shook her head. As their bond had deepened, Armand had shared so much with her about his love for Julia and how he'd spent a lifetime second-guessing his decision to stay in Paris and let her go. "He said nothing to me about this conversation."

"Probably because nothing came of it." Schulz

drew in a breath and let it out. "I met with him at his restaurant. Having purchased a meal, I asked to speak to the chef. He came out to speak to his customer. When I told him the real purpose of my visit, he sat for a few minutes and listened. He said he'd never seen or heard his parents speak of any special artwork. If they had taken it with them when they left their estate, they had sold it along the way. Even if they had left it for him, he had no use for such expensive decoration. He would have sold it to upgrade his restaurant. I believed him. When he died two days later, I began to think the thief that had followed my research had gone from stealing priceless objects to killing those who might currently possess them."

Amelie's gut knotted. She'd been shocked and found it very hard to believe that such a vibrant man, so full of life and passion for his culinary art, could drop dead so suddenly. She'd convinced him to get a physical the year before, and the doctor had given him a squeaky-clean bill of health. How could he suddenly have had a heart problem?

Had Armand been murdered?

A hand reached for hers in her lap. Maurice curled his warm fingers around her cold ones and squeezed gently. He directed his gaze toward

Schulz. "Why wait all this time after Armand's death to come after his son and Ms. Aubert?"

Schulz looked down at his hands. "After I learned of Armand's demise, I stopped searching for the painting. Between the thefts of other artwork I located and Armand's death after I spoke with him, I stepped back from my research and focused on other pursuits. I felt responsible in a way for the death of Armand Benoît and refused to be responsible for leading the killer to others I might interview in my search for her."

Amelie couldn't help but notice Schulz's use of the word *her* in reference to the painting of the *Lady by the Stream*.

"For over two years, I resisted the urge to physically follow the Benoît's journey. Instead, I continued my research online and looked for any evidence of a sale of that painting in the French countryside near where they'd hidden while waiting for a ship to the US. I also looked for any mention of such a sale in New Orleans during the time they lived there."

"Did you find one?" Amelie asked.

"None listing a Claude Monet." His brow furrowed. "Although I didn't find a sale, I found a record from a respected New Orleans art dealer who had performed an appraisal on a painting for an anonymous Frenchman. That appraisal was performed in June of 1945, shortly after the victory in Europe. The notes indicated an impressionist painting. Artist's name was identified by only the initials C.M., with the appraised value of two thousand dollars, which, at that time, was significant, especially considering the cost of funding a world war."

"You think that was the Benoîts' painting?" To Amelie, it made sense.

Schulz nodded. "The information was worth investigating."

"Which would indicate the painting made it to the US," Maurice concluded. "And they didn't sell it. At least, not in New Orleans."

"If Armand had no knowledge of the painting's whereabouts, I would assume you hit a dead-end," Amelie said.

"I would have agreed, except for old letters I discovered on an ancestry website, written by Germaine Benoît to Olivier Lecroix, his distant cousin in Nice, dated before the German occupation of France. In those letters, Benoît warned his cousin that if German occupation of France was imminent, he should hide his assets and record the location in a code, like they used when they'd played secret agents as children. He should place that code in something meaningful to him but not to anyone else."

Maurice's brow furrowed. "What's meaningful to you but not to anyone else?"

"A personal journal would mean a lot to yourself and not to anyone else."

Amelie's lips twisted. "Unless your life was more interesting." She didn't recall seeing any journals in Armand's possessions. However, he could have stored them away.

Photographs of family members were another medium meaningful only to those who cared about the people in them.

Amelie almost spoke but then bit down on her tongue instead. Luis had Armand's old photographs. Though Schulz was leading them to believe someone else was following him around and stealing the items he'd located, Amelie wasn't ready to trust the man.

And then there was the watch. She wanted to look at Maurice but resisted. Once Schulz left, she would share her thoughts with him and give Luis a call.

"Again, if you were researching online, why did you decide to get out and put boots on the ground?"

Schulz sighed. "An acquaintance I know at the

U.S. National Archives and Records Administration, who knew I'd spent a lot of time with the files containing the artworks, sent a text, letting me know the photo album containing the *Lady by the Stream* had been stolen a week ago." His brow furrowed. "I suspect whoever took it could be connected to Armand Benoît's untimely demise." He met Amelie's gaze.

"Why would he take three years to show up looking for more clues?" Maurice asked.

"Like me, he might have turned to online research. The letters I found were posted recently. The search then went from the actual painting to a document or journal with a code that could lead to the painting."

"In essence, a treasure map," Amelie said softly.

Schulz nodded.

"As I told you before, Armand lived a simple life outside the restaurant," Amelie said. "He left little behind—just money he set up in a trust for his son."

"No journals, ledgers, books or letters he might have had in his library or had his attorney deliver upon his death?" Schulz asked.

Amelie's lips pressed together. "His work at the restaurant was everything to him." He'd been happiest in his element, making great cuisine.

"I came to warn you to beware." Schulz pushed to his feet and straightened his blazer.

Maurice and Amelie rose as well.

"I shall be in New Orleans to check on shipping industry documentation, on the slim chance they keep records that far back of Germaine's employment," Schulz said. "I hope to locate the residence where the Benoîts lived."

"If the house still exists," Maurice said. "Hurricane Katrina and the resulting flooding destroyed a significant portion of some of the older neighborhoods."

"I am aware." Schulz held out his hand to Amelie. "Thank you for your time and patience."

"Good luck on your search."

Maurice shook his hand next. "Let us know if you find anything. Now that we know what's at stake, we're curious about the final destination of the Monet."

The other man nodded. "She deserves to shine in the light." He turned and left the diner.

Mandy Boudreaux, the black-haired, brown-eyed young woman who'd purchased the diner from Tante Mimi, thus becoming the new Mimi, hurried over with a pot of coffee. "Need a refill?"

Amelie pushed her coffee cup closer. "Hit me, Mimi."

"I'll take some of that as well," Maurice said.

As she poured, Mimi murmured, "That looked like one intense conversation. Everything all right?"

Amelie smiled at her friend and peer. Mimi, a talented chef in her own right, had left New Orleans for the quieter life in Bayou Mambaloa. On several occasions, they'd teamed up to cater events in the area. "As all right as it can be."

"I'm sorry about what happened to the bakery. What I don't understand is who would anyone ransack a bakery and leave without taking some of your mouth-watering pastries?"

Amelie grinned. "Someone on a diet?"

"What's wrong with people?" Mimi poured coffee into Maurice's cup. "You let me know if you need anything over there. And I'll keep an eye out for anyone lurking." Mimi reached out to take Amelie's hand with her empty one. "Neighbors have to look out for each other."

Amelie's eyes filled, and her heart swelled. "Thanks, Mimi. Moving back to Mambaloa was the best decision I ever made."

"Same here," Mimi said. "Who needs a big city where you're surrounded by people you don't know?"

A customer called out, "Mimi, I could use some of that coffee over here."

"That's my cue." Mimi grinned. "Be careful out there."

As soon as Mimi left their table, Amelie brought out her cell phone.

Maurice shifted to sit across from her. "Calling Luis?" he asked in a low tone only she could hear.

She nodded.

In a whisper, he added, "About the photos?"

Again, she nodded, selected Luis's number and placed the call.

Luis answered on the first ring. "You must be a mind reader."

She laughed. "Were you thinking about me?"

"Not only was I thinking about you, but I was also just packing an overnight bag."

Amelie smiled. "Are you coming to Bayou Mambaloa?"

"If the offer's still open, I'd like to come tomorrow."

"Always."

"Good, then I'll see you tomorrow."

"Wait," Amelie said before he could hang up. "Luis, can you look at the backs of your father's photos?"

"I guess," he said. "Why?"

"Just to see if there's anything written on them."

"Give me a minute. I'll have to pull them out of their frames," Luis said. "I'll be right back."

Amelie's gaze met Maurice's.

He reached across the table and took her empty hand, his fingers curling around hers, grounding her and making her remember to breathe.

"I'm back," Luis said. "I'm looking at the backs of the photographs. On the one taken in their first home in Paris, their names, Germaine and Celine Benoît, are handwritten with the date of May the third, 1940."

"Anything else?" Amelie asked.

"No." He paused. "On the one taken in front of the Saint Louis Cathedral, there's just the date of October 14, 1950."

Amelie had hoped to find more than just dates and names. If the photos didn't have a secret code on them, Germaine's idea to hide the directions to valuable assets could be lost forever in a book or journal that had been donated to the homeless. Monet's painting could be hidden somewhere, never to be found.

"Is that all you needed?" Luis asked.

"It is," Amelie responded, masking her disappointment.

"I'll bring the photos with me in case you want to inspect them yourself."

"Thanks, Luis. Drive safely. The roads in the bayou can be a little tricky. We'll see you tomorrow." After the call ended, Amelie's mouth twisted in a wry smile. "Well, scratch the photos. Where else would Germaine have hidden the code that would lead to his assets?"

Maurice squeezed her hand gently. "We might never find out."

"Seems a shame for the painting to be lost forever. I would love to have seen it in all its glorious color."

"It seems others would love to see it as well."

Amelie shivered. "Do you believe Fredrick's story?"

Maurice's eyes narrowed. "If he's right, someone is hellbent on finding that painting and isn't above killing to get there first."

"Do you think that someone is Schulz, trying to throw us off by making us think it's someone else?" Amelie's fingers tightened around Maurice's.

"I feel like the alligators are circling the swamp."

"If it's all the same to you, I'll stay in the boat with you."

CHAPTER 8

MAURICE INSISTED on taking their uneaten dinner with them. "We'll be hungry later."

"I have food in my refrigerator," Amelie argued.

He cocked an eyebrow. "Yogurt and salad?"

She grimaced. "Yeah, but it's healthier than burgers and fries."

"I'll take the burger and fries. You can have the yogurt and salad."

Mimi brought the container and their bill.

When Amelie reached for the check, Maurice snatched it away before she could get her fingers around it. "My treat."

"But it's your job to protect me, not to pay for my meals," she said. "At least let me pay for half."

"You can get the next one. Especially since you probably won't be eating this hamburger anyway."

"You have a point." She nodded. "I'll get the next one."

He liked the idea of sharing another meal with the pretty baker. "By the way, having dinner with you doesn't feel like part of the job."

Her cheeks flushed a pretty pink. "Is that a good thing?"

"Absolutely. At least for me." He slid the burgers into the container and dumped all the fries in with them. "Ready?"

She nodded. "I could use a good night's sleep. I'm sure you can, too. Are you sure you don't want to go to your room in the boarding house tonight?"

Had she lost her mind?

"After Schulz's warning, I'm sticking to you like gum on a hot sidewalk," he said with a wink.

Amelie laughed out loud, then snorted. She slapped a hand over her nose and mouth, her eyes wide.

He touched his hand to her cheek. "Glad to see you can laugh. You should do it more often."

"Minus the snort, maybe," she agreed.

"No," he said. "Keep the snort."

"Gum on a hot sidewalk?" She chuckled and hooked her hand through the crook of his arm as they left the diner.

They'd walked to the diner before the sun had

set. During the time they'd been inside, dark had since settled over Bayou Mambaloa. Cicadas and frogs had begun their nightly rivalry, battling to be the loudest creatures of the night.

Maurice shook his head. "Anyone who thinks they're moving to the country for peace and quiet hasn't lived in the bayou."

"I like the sound. It's like the steady hum of life after the town rolls up its sidewalks for the night." She leaned into Maurice and let her hand slide down to grasp his.

For a moment, he stiffened, realizing she was on his right side and the hand she'd reached for was severely scarred and missing a finger. The one mutilated by phosphorus in a battle where he'd failed to save his fiancée and had subsequently ended his career.

Amelie didn't flinch from the texture of his scars. She held his damaged hand as if it were the same as the undamaged one and continued walking alongside him.

When she didn't react, he relaxed. Through all the work they'd done together to restore the bakery after the break-in, she'd never treated him as if he were disabled or incapable of doing anything a man with two normal hands could do.

Other women had recoiled at the ugly scars. Not Amelie.

With no pressing deadline, no reason to hurry, Maurice was content to take his time walking the few blocks. He walked slowly down Main Street toward the bakery, marveling at how different it was from all the other times he'd walked down the same street over the past two years. He felt a sense of belonging. Like this was his town. Bayou Mambaloa was becoming his home.

What had changed?

It was the same street. The same shops and businesses. The same diner, bakery and yoga studio he'd passed hundreds of times before.

That night, the difference wasn't where he was but who he was with.

Yes, he'd known Amelie as the baker who made the best pastries he'd ever had. Until he'd offered to see her home from the Crawdad Hole, he hadn't really known the woman behind the Baked with Love apron.

She was smart and sexy, a baker, chef, business-woman and entrepreneur.

More than that, she welcomed strangers into her bakery like family, eager to smile and talk with them. She lived her logo and baked everything with love. Love for the process. Love for the combination of ingredients and love for the people who would enjoy the finished products.

Just being around her energy, optimism and gregarious personality made Maurice feel more alive than he had in a long time. Like the sun had finally pushed through the clouds.

When they climbed the steps to her apartment, Amelie paused before unlocking the door. "Thank you for helping me get my shop in order so quickly and for dinner tonight."

He held up the container. "A dinner you didn't eat."

She smiled up at him, starlight reflecting off her eyes. "I had a few bites." She laid a hand on his chest and lowered her voice. "How about we warm up...the leftovers and...finish what we started?"

Her words melted into his soul like honey on a hot biscuit. His mind shot past the food in his hand to the kiss she'd initiated the night before. Maurice's gaze dropped from her eyes to her lips, and all logic evaporated like rain in the desert.

"Screw the leftovers," he growled, as he dropped the container, gathered her in his arms and crushed her mouth with his.

Her hands on his chest slid up to lace behind

his head, bringing him closer, her breasts pressing against his chest.

When he traced the seam of her lips, she opened and met his tongue with hers in a searing caress. Maurice forgot where he was, forgot the world around him and how to breathe.

When his body reminded him that air was good, he raised his head and dragged in a deep breath.

Amelie leaned her forehead against his chest, her fingers curling into his shirt. "I lied."

He chuckled and tucked a strand of her hair behind her ear. "About what?"

"I told you I wouldn't try to kiss you again."

"And yet, you did."

She leaned back, her pretty brow furrowing. "Look. I'm attracted to you, and I think you're attracted to me."

Maurice couldn't help himself. He brushed his lips across hers. "I think that was obvious the last time this happened."

She poked a finger at his chest. "You're not into commitment, and I'm totally okay with that. So, what's keeping us from having unfettered, gratuitous sex?"

When Maurice opened his mouth to respond, Amelie pressed her finger to his lips.

"Don't try to make things complicated. It's just sex."

He bit the tip of her finger, fisted his good hand in her hair and leaned down until his lips hovered over hers. "I have a feeling that making love with you will never be just sex, and everything about what I feel when I'm with you is destined to be complicated."

"Less talk." She hooked her hand around the back of his neck. "More action."

Then he was kissing her again, desperate to chase the shadows of the past from the present with her. When he came up again for air, his pulse thundered through his veins, driving heat to his extremities. Instantly hard, he pressed her back to the door and leaned the evidence of his desire into her belly. "And yes, I'm attracted to you."

"Oh, good." She laughed breathlessly. "I've wanted to do that since last time." When she raised her face to him, her hand slipped the key into his. "Can we take this inside?"

He palmed the key and leaned in for a quick brush of his lips across hers as he fit the key in the lock like he wanted to fit his cock inside her.

He twisted the key, shoved open the door and swung her inside. Once over the threshold, he kicked the door shut behind them.

What had started as a peaceful walk along Main Street quickly escalated into a frenzy of motion as they stripped off their clothing while crossing the living room floor.

Maurice yanked off his T-shirt, toed off his boots and ripped open the line of buttons on his jeans.

His breath caught and held as Amelie shoved her jeans over her hips and down to her ankles. She stepped free and kicked them into a corner. Then she backed toward the bedroom with her hand on the hem of her shirt. "Are you coming?" she teased. In brutally slow motion, she dragged the shirt up and over her head and flung it toward Maurice.

Standing in only her bra and panties, she reached behind her back and released the hooks on her bra. As the straps slid down her arms, she raised her hands to hold the cups in place.

Then she spun, dropped the bra, raced for the bed and leaped into the middle, laughing.

Maurice followed at a slightly slower pace and stopped as she rolled to her side, exposing her naked breasts, so plump and tempting.

She traced one of her fingers across her hip, stopping to tug at the elastic band of her string-bikini panties. "See?" she said, her voice husky and sexy as hell. "Completely uncomplicated."

"Oh, sweetheart, you have complicated written all over you." One determined step at a time, he closed the distance between them. He halted near the bed, pulled his wallet out of his back pocket, plucked a condom from inside and tossed both the wallet and the condom packet on the nightstand.

Amelie gave him a saucy wink and dragged the elastic over her hip and down her thigh. "I'll even remove the strings, if you like." Every move, every expression taunted him, coaxed him, enticed him to take what she so freely and joyfully offered.

The guilt, having faded over the years, finally eased, releasing him from the chains of his failure and loss. "We're really doing this, aren't we?"

Amelie's eyes narrowed as she studied him, a hand coming up to cover one breast. "If that's what you want."

"Oh, I want," he said, his body on fire with need and raging desire.

When he continued to hesitate, she swung her legs over the side of the bed, reached for the waist-band of his jeans and slid her hands between the denim and his butt cheeks. "Are you sure? Or do you need a little more convincing?" Her hands closed around his cheeks and squeezed. Then she pushed his jeans off his hips, slid the denim down his thighs, her hands caressing his legs on the way down.

As Maurice kicked the jeans aside, Amelie skimmed her hands back up the inside of his thighs to capture his dick between her palms.

Maurice sucked in a breath and held it, heart thudding in his chest, adrenaline screaming through his veins. Every fiber of his being raged for him to drive right into her and ride her hard, fast and completely.

Amelie had other, more subtle yet wickedly delicious ideas. Her hands moved along his length, strong and supple, coaxing a response though no coaxing was needed.

Maurice's body responded, his muscles tensing with every stroke.

When Amelie leaned forward and sucked him into her mouth, he fisted his hand in her dark hair and fought for restraint.

Her fingers fondled his balls and then slipped over his hips to grasp his buttocks. She pulled him toward her, taking him in, her teeth lightly scraping his length.

When the tip of his shaft bumped the back of her throat, his breath hitched, and his control took a hit. He froze in place until he could master control again and then slid almost all the way out.

Amelie took over, bringing him back in, then out. Again. And again, until Maurice's body took over and set the pace with an immediate increase in speed and thrust.

With his good hand tangled in her hair, he pumped in and out, taking his senses to the very edge.

Before he lost it, he pulled free, turned Amelie over and bent her across the bed, her legs draped over the side.

He leaned over her, his rock-hard cock nudging the crease between her butt cheeks. As he reached beneath her and fondled her breasts, he slid his dick between her legs to tap her entrance.

He wanted nothing more than to plunge into her. To take her hard, fast and completely.

Before he did, though, he wanted her to come first.

He leaned back, pressed a kiss to her ass, rolled her to her back and scooted her up on the mattress.

Maurice climbed up over her, settled his legs between hers and leaned down to take her mouth in a slow, searing kiss.

Amelie brought her knees up on either side of

Maurice's hips and squeezed them together, locking him in for a moment.

He chuckled against her lips, kissed them and then trailed his lips across her jaw and down the length of her throat.

Moving lower, he skimmed across her collarbone and down to one luscious, full breast. Maurice cupped it with his palm and flicked the nipple with the tip of his tongue.

She sucked in a breath and moaned, her chest rising toward him.

He flicked it again, teasing the rosy flesh into a tight little peak. Satisfied with the one, he switched to the other and sucked it into his mouth, flicking the nipple until it matched the first.

Amelie's fingers curled around the back of his neck, holding him close as he slipped lower, kissing a gentle path down her torso, touching each rib on his way to the prize.

Her body tensed as he cupped her sex in his palm and slid a finger into her hot, wet channel. She sucked in a shaky breath and moaned his name, "Maurice."

"Want me to stop?" he asked.

Her hips bucked. "Don't," she gasped. "Stop. Please. I'm on fire."

Maurice slipped his hands beneath her

buttocks and used his thumbs to part her folds, baring her glistening pussy to him.

She was so wet. So ready.

Knowing he'd done that to her made his cock even harder. He wanted her. But more than that, he wanted to make her as crazy for him as he was for her. He wanted her to come before he sank into her and slaked his own desires.

Maurice dipped a finger into her channel and swirled in her juices. With his wet finger, he gently stroked her clit, moving slowly at first, then increasing the speed with each pass until she writhed against the sheets.

But she wasn't quite there. He wanted her so lost in the moment that she came with full abandon.

He blew a stream of air over her heated core and then closed his mouth over her, sucking her clit between his lips.

She gasped, bucked and moaned. Her fingers dug into his scalp. Her hips rose from the mattress, and her back arched.

She was close.

Maurice could feel the tension build in her body. When he flicked her clit again, she cried out, "Oh, sweet Jesus! I can't breathe."

He lifted his head, afraid he'd somehow hurt her.

Her fingers dug into his scalp, urging him back to the task. "For the love of—" she said raggedly, "Don't. Stop!"

He complied, his tongue stroking her at her most sensitive spot until her body jerked, she stiffened and she rode her release all the way to the last flick of his tongue.

Amelie dropped back to the mattress and flung her arms out to her sides. "Am I dead?"

Maurice chuckled. "No, you're quite alive."

"I swear I died and floated all the way to heaven."

"Well, welcome back." Maurice climbed up her body and kissed her lips.

She opened her eyes and stared up into his, their faces warm in the glow of the lamplight. "You're not stopping now, are you?"

He couldn't stop now. Watching her lose herself only made him want her more. But it was her choice. "It's up to you."

"Don't stop. I believe I have another orgasm in me, and I want to have it," she leaned up and brushed his lips, "with yours."

His cock twitched with impatience. Maurice leaned across, grabbed the condom and tore it open.

Amelie took it from him and rolled it over his straining member. Then she guided him to her.

His body thrummed with the need to plunge inside her slick entrance. He remained poised for launch, counted to five and fought to regain control. Otherwise, he'd blow his wad like a teenager having sex with a girl for his first time.

Before he reached five, her hands gripped his hips and drove him home. All the way. Fully sheathed. Surrounded by warm, wet muscles, contracting around his length.

Drawing in a deep breath, he began to move in and out, gaining speed with each pass. Soon, he pumped like the piston in a sports car.

The bed rocked so hard the headboard smacked the wall.

Amelie wrapped her legs around him and pressed her heels into his ass. "Faster, soldier," she gasped. "So damned...close. Yes. Oh, yes. There!"

Tension stretched his muscles tight as energy built, expanded and finally shot him over the edge. He plunged once...twice. On the third thrust, he sank deep, held steady and surfed the waves of his orgasm all the way to the last throb, the last vibration of his cock.

Amelie's feet dropped to the mattress, her knees splaying to the sides, her body going limp.

Maurice lowered himself onto her, lying skin to skin, their bodies hot and slick with sweat.

Concerned he was crushing her, he rolled with her onto their sides and held her close, not ready to sever their intimate connection.

After a while, he pressed a kiss to her temple. "Are you okay?"

"Mmmm," she hummed. "Better than okay. You?"

He closed his eyes and smiled. "I swear I died and went all the way to heaven."

Amelie chuckled. "Welcome back." She nestled her cheek into his chest and sighed. "And don't worry... I'm not a clinger."

Maurice frowned. "Clinger?"

"One of those clingy women who thinks that sex means commitment. If you walk out that door tonight, I won't chase after you or ask why you didn't call. It's just sex."

With her warm curves pressed against his body, his cock still rooted inside her, Maurice couldn't comprehend her words.

Just sex?

Oh, fuck no.

Then what was it?

And was he ready to do anything about it?

He lay still for a long moment without responding, his thoughts pinging through his brain's synapses like rogue balls in a pinball machine.

One thought emerged from the chaos.

He wanted to make love to her again. And no—it was not *just sex*.

CHAPTER 9

Amelie dragged herself out of bed at three-thirty the next morning, foggy-eyed and sore in all the right places. She didn't regret the loss of sleep, only that the night hadn't been longer and she'd promised the Broussards she'd bring fresh bread and pastries to sell in their store. Big mistake.

Note to self. Monday is your day off. Make no promises for your day off.

They'd gone for round two after hamburgers and yogurt and a desperate search for another condom. Maurice found one buried deep in his wallet behind an emergency one-hundred-dollar bill. If he'd had more condoms, not hundreds, they'd have kept going all the way until time for her to get up and get to work.

After gathering her clothes, Amelie tiptoed into the bathroom and eased the door closed. Only then did she turn on the light and risk a glance at herself in the mirror.

Her dark hair stood out at all angles in glorious tangles. Her neck sported a red beard rash from Maurice's five-o'clock shadow, and she looked like she'd had fillers injected in her lips because they were so swollen from kissing that gorgeous man lying naked in her bed.

She raised her fingers to her lips and stared at the woman in the reflection, wondering who she was with the radiant glow of a woman who'd experienced the best sex of her entire life.

She had to remind herself to enjoy it while it lasted. After all, it was *just sex*.

No strings besides those on her bikini panties and none of that C-word... Commitment.

It was hard enough to find a man who wanted a forever partner. Amelie wasn't even sure how one would compete with a ghost to secure Maurice's affection.

Her chest tightened.

Maurice must have been deeply in love with his fiancée to be still grieving her after so many years.

She must have been special.

Amelie realized she wanted to know more about her. She'd been such a big part of Maurice's life. Their time together had helped shape him into the man he was today.

With a sigh, she went to work on her hair, easing out the tangles so that she could pull it back in the requisite ponytail that kept it out of her way and out of the food. Too tired to worry about makeup, she splashed cool water on her face, brushed her teeth, pulled on the sundress she'd chosen to wear for the day and slipped her feet into strappy sandals. She allowed herself a brief glance in the full-length mirror, knowing full well she'd dressed nicer than usual because of him.

They would be friends with benefits until one or the other decided the benefits were no longer necessary.

Still, it didn't hurt to show him a little of what he'd be missing should he decide the benefits were no longer a thing.

As for Amelie, she didn't want the friends-with-benefits perks to end anytime soon. After a number of dry years with no more sex than what she provided herself with her battery-powered boyfriend, she found that a living, breathing, full-bodied man was so much better.

And if he made her feel safe and protected and was fun to be with, even when they weren't banging the headboard—*bonus*. Her battery-powered boyfriend couldn't hold up his end of a conversation. All he did was hum.

Amelie touched the red beard burn on her neck and sighed. She'd have to be satisfied with whatever time they had together. Once the danger was past, Maurice would have no reason to hang out with her. They might see each other passing on the street. It was a small town.

He might eventually move past his grief and find a woman who made him happy.

Then Amelie could wave at the couple shopping for engagement rings or baby furniture. She'd be all right with that, wouldn't she?

A stab of something that felt like jealousy jabbed her in the gut.

Oh, hell no.

In their short time in close quarters, he'd gotten under her skin. Though she'd assured him it was *just sex*, it wasn't. Not to her, anyway.

That thought shook her to the core. She froze with her hand on the doorknob, afraid to open the bathroom door. Afraid he'd be awake and see what she was feeling reflected in her eyes or the way she moved around him.

A knock on the door made her jump.

"Amelie? Are you all right in there?"

"Yes," she squeaked, cleared her throat and tried again. "I'm fine." She dragged in a steadying breath, let it out, pasted a smile on her face and flung open the door.

He stood there, bare-chested, wearing his jeans, though he hadn't bothered to button them.

With every intention of ducking past him, she stepped forward.

Maurice took her hands and pulled her into his arms, tipped her chin up and brushed his lips across hers. "Got time for a quickie?" he murmured against her ear.

She laughed shakily, her body instantly humming with desire. "We used the last condom," she reminded him.

"Don't need a condom to get you there," he whispered in her ear and nibbled on her lobe.

Lost in a haze of lust, she closed her eyes. Her head fell back automatically, giving him full access to her neck. He accepted the invitation, trailing his lips downward to the junction of her neck and shoulder. "What's this? A dress? Mmm." He slid his fingers beneath the spaghetti strap and pushed it off her shoulder. Then he worked the other one until it fell around her elbow.

"I should get down to the kitch—" Amelie's breath snagged in her lungs as he tugged the front of her dress down below her breasts and captured one in his palm.

He bent to tease the nipple until it puckered into a tight little button.

Her hands rose automatically to weave into the hair at the back of his head, pressing him closer.

Maurice bent, caught the backs of her thighs and lifted.

She wrapped her legs around his waist, her sex riding the mound beneath his denim fly as he carried her back into the bathroom and sat her on the edge of the counter.

"Have you ever worked all day wearing a dress?" he asked, his mouth moving over her breast while his hand slid under her skirt.

"Y-yes," she faltered as his finger nudged her panties to the side and slid into her.

God, she was already so hot and wet. She wanted him inside her, making use of the lubricant her body produced in excess when he touched her like that.

Maurice hooked the elastic and dragged the panties down her legs and off, then tucked them into his jeans pocket. Then he dropped to his knees, lifted her skirt, draped her legs over his shoulders and went under.

Resistance was futile when he did the things he did to her down there—licking, sucking and thrusting into her with his tongue. But when he focused on her clit, he slayed her, sending shock waves throughout her body and making her tremble with the force of her release.

She clung to him, too shaken by the intensity of the sensations to form coherent thoughts, much less words.

When he finally surfaced, she slumped against him, murmuring, "I'm buying stock in condoms."

He laughed and gathered her into his arms. "It'll be an excellent investment. I can see us needing a warehouse full of supplies at this rate."

Her arms were still shaking as she struggled to adjust her dress.

Maurice brushed her hands aside, tugged the bodice over her breasts, pausing briefly to tweak her pebbled nipples. He swept the straps up over her shoulders and cupped her face in his palm. "I never knew three-thirty in the morning could be this good."

"It's never been this good. You've completely moved the bar." She laid her hands on his shoulders as he helped her off the counter to stand on her feet.

"If you're done in here, I'll only be a minute," he said, holding the door for her to exit.

She held out her hand. "My panties?"

His eyebrows rose then fell. "Consider them payment. Better yet, a reminder of that bar we set." He patted his pocket. "Plus, it'll prolong the arousal as you work without them."

Her eyes widened. "I can't do that. This dress is too short. What if it rides up? What if someone comes in?"

"You said yourself that the shop is closed on Monday. It'll be our secret." He gave her a gentle nudge, sending her over the threshold into the bedroom. "And no cheating."

Amelie stood in her bedroom, her body still thrumming from her orgasm, cool air flowing over her private parts beneath her skirt.

How was she supposed to get any work done when all she wanted to do was mount Maurice and ride him all day long?

She marched over to her dresser and opened the top drawer where she kept her panties neatly folded. She stared down at the silky scraps that barely covered anything, her girly parts still throbbing from her release.

She pushed the drawer in and left the bedroom. In the kitchenette, she opened the refrigerator, pulled out a small can of apple juice, tucked it beneath her dress and pressed it to her sex, willing the fire to abate to a point at which her brain might engage.

When the door in the other room creaked open, she almost dropped the can. She quickly rinsed it off and put it back in the refrigerator. This was insane. If she were a man, she'd have a continuous hard-on. She couldn't function like this.

Maurice appeared in the doorway, wearing his boots and carrying his T-shirt. His jeans still hung open, exposing a tempting amount of pubic hair, and was that the velvety tip of his erection?

"Are you going commando?" she asked.

He dragged the shirt over his head and down his torso. "Does that bother you?"

"N-no," she stuttered.

"That's a shame." He tucked his T-shirt into the waistband of his jeans, adjusted his package and secured the buttons, effectively blocking her view. "Are you ready?"

She nodded, eager to leave the intimacy of her apartment. Surely, she'd get her head on straight in the bakery kitchen.

Maurice was first out onto the landing, looking both ways before he allowed her out of the door. He rested a hand against the small of her back as they descended the stairs.

The cool night air wafted up beneath her skirt, reminding her with every step that she was naked down there. He was right. Everything about it felt racy, decadent and dangerous and kept her blood stirring.

Once in the kitchen, she preheated the ovens and pulled the trays she'd prepped the night before from the refrigerator.

While she worked, Maurice moved around the shop with a clean, damp rag, touching up, straightening chairs and wiping fingerprints off the display cases they'd missed the day before.

Several times, she caught him staring at her, a smile pulling at the corners of his lips as if he knew her secret.

And he did.

Each time, her core heated, and her pulse quickened.

The sooner she finished the baking and delivered the product to Broussard's, the sooner she could buy more condoms. Monday was her day off. She could do whatever she wanted to, including spending the day in bed.

With Maurice.

If he was willing.

Based on the smoldering glances he was sending her way, he was willing.

Once the bread and pastries were baked, bagged and tagged, Maurice helped her load them into the delivery van. The sun was just rising as they closed the back door and rounded to the front.

She held out her hand. "I'm not leaving without you know what."

His lips curved in a smile. "Let me guess. Your mother told you always to wear clean underwear in case you got into an accident."

Her cheeks heated. "Exactly." She wiggled her fingers. "Give me."

With a sigh, he pulled the panties from his pocket. "Can't go against a mother's loving rule." He held out the panties.

She reached for them, but he snatched them back. "Did you learn anything from your morning working while going commando beneath your dress?"

"Yes." She lunged for his hand, snagged the undergarment and darted away. "Never trust a man who gives you an orgasm and steals your panties."

She stepped into the panties in front of him and pulled them up beneath the dress. "Now, I need to get these items to Broussard's before they open for the day."

"Yes, ma'am." Maurice gave her a mock salute. "Just so you know, I've had a hard-on all morning knowing I had your panties and you didn't."

No man had the right to be as sexy as Maurice Boucher.

Amelie's sex clenched. Alan Broussard had better have a huge stock of condoms, or she'd be in deep trouble for the rest of her day off.

And he did.

After they deposited the pastries and bread, Amelie shopped for a few necessities, including a dozen eggs, a beef roast, baking potatoes and fresh salad ingredients. She slipped into the toiletries aisle at the last minute, searching for a big box of protection.

Having left Maurice talking with Alan Broussard, Amelie figured she had a few minutes alone to find what she needed and slip it into her cart.

"The ribbed ones give the woman more pleasure. Of course, the man couldn't care less as long as he's protected from paternity suits."

Amelie spun, heat filling her cheeks as she faced Chrissy Brousard, mother of six Alan Broussard's wife and Amelie's friend Shelby's older sister. "Hey, Chrissy. How's the little one?"

Alan's pretty bride held her sixth child cradled in her arms, barely four months old and suckling at her breast barely concealed beneath a light blanket. She smiled. "Trust me. You want as much pleasure as you can get before you're swimming in babies and never get a whole night's sleep to yourself."

Amelie had always admired how Chrissy juggled motherhood and business ownership like a champ. Her children might not always be as well put together as their mother, Chrissy, but they had clothes on their backs, a roof over their heads and healthy food to help them grow big and strong.

"Um. I was just looking for some ointment for a rash I might have." She reached for a tube of hydrocortisone.

"Honey, don't let embarrassment keep you from protecting yourself and your future. Your choice to be with a man shouldn't be because you didn't take the proper precautions, and now you can't afford to raise a child on your own. Women should never have to rely on a man to help them raise a child. They should be in a position to raise a child on their own."

Her cheeks still burning, Amelie looked away.

"I would never abandon a child because I made a bad call sleeping with his father."

Chrissy's face relaxed, and she chuckled. "I'm giving you a hard time when I should be helping you celebrate good times."

Amelie frowned. "What good times? Someone broke into my bakery. I had to trash all the ingredients I've collected all these years, close my shop and conduct a massive cleaning effort as well as restocking shelves."

Chrissy grimaced.

Amelie snorted softly. "That's no reason to celebrate."

"No, but I recognize the glow of a woman well loved." She picked up a box of condoms and added them to Amelie's basket. "Celebrate, sweetie. Maurice is one of the good guys."

"We're just friends," Amelie blurted and added in a whisper, "with benefits. While it lasts."

"Whatever melts your butter, sweetie. At the beginning of a relationship, you don't know how long it'll last. But if the sex ain't good, it'll be over after the first night." She nodded toward the box. "Based on your priorities, I'd say this one has a chance." She winked and grinned. The baby on her breast pulled free of the nipple with a loud popping sound." Without missing a beat, Chrissy adjusted her blouse, kissed the fuzz on the baby's head and headed for the counter where her husband and Maurice were still talking.

Amelie had hoped that by the time she finished her shopping, the men would have moved on, leaving her to check out with Chrissy. It was one thing to get advice from another woman, but she didn't want to pull out the box of condoms in front of the two men.

As she approached, Chrissy's eyes narrowed. "Alan, have you shown Maurice the new fishing poles that arrived yesterday?"

Alan turned to Maurice. "I understand you like fishing in the bayou."

Maurice nodded. "I do. Mitch has taken me out on occasion to show me some of the good spots to drop a line."

"Then you might be interested in the shipment of rigs we received yesterday." Alan led Maurice to a display on the far side of the store.

Amelie gave Chrissy a grateful mile. "Thanks."

"Women like to take care of business, but we don't always want to advertise."

Chrissy laid her baby in a bouncy seat behind the counter and rang up Amelie's purchases. She had placed the last of her items in a bag when Alan and Maurice rejoined them.

"Ready?" Maurice asked.

Before Amelie could answer, the bell over the entrance door rang, announcing the arrival of customers.

LaShawnda Jones, Bayou Mambaloa's most successful real estate agent, made an entrance, as was usual for her. Dressed in a bright orange fitted skirt suit that complemented her smooth, cocoa-colored skin, she strode through the door, her matching orange stilettos clicking against the tile.

Amelie envied the realtor's daring style, color choices and absolute confidence.

Along with her eye-popping orange attire, she wore shiny gold, chunky jewelry around her wrists and neck, and huge gold hoops dangled from her ears. She paused just inside the doorway and turned to the man entering behind her.

Because she owned the bakery, Amelie was familiar with all the locals who called Bayou Mambaloa home. She didn't recognize this guy and assumed he was new to town. He wore what appeared to be a tailor-made suit that fit him to perfection and shiny black, patent-leather shoes.

"Good morning," LaShawnda called out as she approached the counter. "I was just showing *Monsieur* Peltier around Bayou Mambaloa and wanted him to see for himself how well-stocked the Broussards keep the shelves." She turned to her client. "Monsieur Eugene Peltier, I'm pleased to introduce you to Alan and Chrissy Broussard."

Alan held out his hand. "Nice to meet you."

Peltier's head dipped as he grasped Alan's hand. "The pleasure is mine," he said with a rich French accent.

Amelie's ears perked. After three years in Louisiana, with the Cajun accent so prevalent in the bayou, hearing a man speak with a true French accent brought back memories of living in Paris.

Chrissy held out her hand.

Peltier had already turned his attention to Maurice.

Chrissy dropped her arm to her side, her lips forming a thin line.

LaShawnda waved a hand toward Maurice. "And this is Maurice Boucher."

Maurice held out his hand.

The man started to take it, but hesitated when his gaze took in the scarring and missing finger.

Maurice lowered his arm, his lips twisting slightly. "Welcome to Bayou Mambaloa."

"*Merci*," the stranger said and turned to Amelie. "And who is this?"

LaShawnda waved her hand with a flourish.

"None other than the owner of Baked with Love, the best bakery in all of Louisiana, Amelie Aubert."

When he took Amelie's hand, he didn't shake it but lifted it and pressed a kiss to the backs of her knuckles. "*Enchanté.*"

Amelie fought the urge to yank back her hand. The man had ignored Chrissy and now felt he could take liberties with her hand.

Who the hell did this freak think he was?

CHAPTER 10

MAURICE MOVED CLOSER, his hand going to the small of her back.

When Peltier didn't release her hand immediately, Amelie pulled it free and moved it behind her back.

Maurice placed his hand over hers, not holding it down but letting her know he was there.

"What brings you to Bayou Mambaloa, Eugene?" Maurice asked, his tone a bit more abrupt than usual. "You don't mind if I call you Eugene, do you?" He didn't really care if Peltier liked it or not.

Peltier dipped his head stiffly. "*S'il vous plaît.* I am what you would call a cultural preservationist interested in learning more about the French influence in New Orleans and the Cajun culture."

"Monsieur Peltier is considering Bayou Mambaloa as his base of operations during his research," LaShawnda said, smiling brightly at the Frenchman. "Since I've served the real estate needs of the community for so long, he asked me to show him around the area. He might decide to set up an office here to work out of."

"How long have you been a cultural preservationist, Monsieur Peltier?" Chrissy asked.

"For over thirty years," he said. "I have traveled many places, researching cultures practically lost through the years. I have followed clues left by those who came before us to relics hidden away in the past to protect them from being destroyed by new regimes."

"How long do you think you'll be in this area?" Alan asked. "We're a relatively young country. You might get bored with a lack of centuries-old history to dig through."

"I never know how long it will take me to complete my research. A day, a week..." He shrugged. "I spent two years following clues I had found hidden among the pages of *The History of the Decline and Fall of the Roman Empire*. They led me to a cave in Portugal."

"Did you find what you were looking for there?" Alan asked.

Peltier's eyes narrowed. "I did not, but it gave me more clues to use in my search."

"I'm sure your life must be very interesting," Amelie said, "compared to life in Bayou Mambaloa."

"Speaking of interesting…" LaShawnda said. "We were going to stop at the bakery for a pastry, but I forgot that you're closed on Monday."

Amelie shot a smile at LaShawnda.

"You can purchase some of her bread and pastries here on Monday, if you like," Alan offered.

"And you're right, LaShawnda," Amelie said with an apologetic grimace. "The bakery is closed on Monday."

"Ms. Jones informed me that you studied the culinary arts in Paris." Peltier cocked an eyebrow. "I am familiar with many of the schools and master chefs in Paris. Where did you study?"

"My initial studies were with Le Cordon Bleu Culinary School, and I interned at *Maison Belle Époque* for a year."

"And after that, you returned to the US to work here?"

Amelie shook her head. "I apprenticed at the *Chez Benoît* for four years before I came home."

Peltier's eyebrows rose. "*Chez Benoît?* I am familiar with the restaurant and the master chef,

Armand Benoît. Did it not close after *Monsieur Benoît's* unfortunate death?"

Amelie nodded, her mouth tightening.

"Such a shame. I had met with *Monsieur Benoît* on occasion. You see, our families were connected. I traced our lineage back and found that his *arrière grand-mère*, how do you say...great grandmother, and mine were close friends. I came across letters in an old trunk in the attic of the family estate in Paris. They were letters my *arrière grand-mère* received from him. Our great-grandmothers grew up together and attended the *Grande Saison* as young debutantes."

"Armand did mention his great-grandmother was active in high society during the eighteen hundreds." Amelie tilted her head and narrowed her eyes. "What did he say her name was?" She tapped her chin. "Was it Anne? No. Anne-Sophie?"

"Yes, yes. Anne-Sophie." Peltier nodded. "They kept in touch, sent gifts at birthdays and Christmas and shared their love of art and music for many years." He sighed with a smile pulling at his lips. "Armand never knew. He did not have the fortune of finding the letters our *arrière grand-mères* exchanged. He did not seem at all interested."

"Armand's life centered around food," Amelie

said. He had never mentioned Peltier. She studied the man's features. "I'm good at remembering faces, if not names. I don't recall seeing you with Armand during the four years I worked closely with him."

"Ah, but then the *Chez Benoît* was very popular. So many people came to Paris just to eat there. How close were you to Armand?"

Amelie shrugged. "As close as a sous chef can be in a kitchen. He was my boss."

Maurice knew Amelie's bond with Armand was much more than an employer-employee relationship. Apparently, she didn't think Peltier needed to know that.

Amelie straightened and lifted her chin. "If you'll excuse me, Monsieur Peltier, it's my day off, and I have a lot to catch up on." She reached for the bags of groceries.

Maurice stepped in front of her. "I'll get them."

"No, thank you," she said. "I'll get them myself." Her eyes met and held his gaze briefly.

Maurice nodded and backed off. The woman wanted to carry her own bags. He suspected it would keep her hands occupied so the Frenchman couldn't repeat the kiss on her knuckles.

"I love a strong, independent woman. And

you're that in spades." He winked, laid a hand to the small of her back and waved as he passed Peltier. "Enjoy your tour of the town."

"Good to see you, LaShawnda," Amelie said as she sailed past.

"Good to see you, too," LaShawnda said with a smile. "I'll be by on Friday for my mother's birthday cake."

"It'll be ready. She's going to love the strawberry filling."

"I know she will," LaShawnda said. "She loves everything that comes out of Baked with Love."

Maurice held the door as Amelie stepped through with her bags.

She marched toward the bakery van, shoved the bags behind her seat and slid behind the wheel.

Maurice climbed into the passenger side, his gaze on her face. "Everything all right?"

Amelie's eyebrows dropped low. "I don't know." She shifted into drive, pulled away from the store and drove down Main Street.

Maurice dug around in the glove box in front of him and found a small plastic bottle of hand sanitizer. "Hold out your hand."

She held out one hand while retaining her grip on the steering wheel with the other. "What is that?"

"Hand sanitizer." He squirted some into her open palm. "If you slow down, I'll hold the wheel."

Amelie gently pressed the brake, slowing the van to under ten miles per hour.

Maurice took the wheel while Amelie rubbed the hand sanitizer between her two hands and over her knuckles.

"Did the French guy give you bad vibes?" Maurice asked, his gaze on the street ahead.

"Yes. And he was lying."

When she took the wheel again, Maurice leaned back in his seat, capped the bottle and stowed it in the glove box. "How so?"

She frowned. "At least, I think he was. I have no idea what Armand's great-grandmother's name was. I made it up. I said the first French female name that came to my mind. Anne-Sophie."

Maurice grinned. "Is that the name of someone you know?"

"I wish," Amelie said. "She's the most famous female chef in the world."

"In the 1800s?"

"No. Today." Amelie shook her head. "I've been following her success story."

"So, Eugene agreed to a fictitious name. Maybe he forgot the real one."

"Or the whole story was a bunch of hooey." Her

brow furrowed. "If he read all his great-grandmother's letters from Armand's great-grandmother, you'd think he'd remember the name. And like I said, I never saw him visit Armand. And Armand never said anything about a Eugene Peltier. For the last three years I worked with Armand, I was his confidant."

Maurice stared out the window. "Why would Peltier make up a story like that?"

"Why would he come all the way from France to Bayou Mambaloa?" Amelie drove the van around to the back of the bakery and parked. "What Frenchman even knows where Bayou Mambaloa is on a map?"

"Even if he didn't visit Armand, he knew who he was." Maurice pushed his door open, grabbed the bags of groceries and followed Amelie. "And he knew you worked in Paris. I suspect he knows your true connection to Armand."

Amelie's lips pressed into a tight line. "Makes me think he came here on purpose."

"To find you." Maurice didn't like that idea.

A box lay on the ground at the back door of the bakery.

Amelie bent to retrieve it and read the label. "Yay. It's the surveillance system I ordered." She glanced up and grinned. "I know what I'll be doing for the rest of the day."

"Good. If we need to, we can get some of my teammates to help us set it up. I want to get it up and operational as soon as possible."

"It's supposed to be easy. I ordered the idiot-proof one."

"Then, between the two of us, we should be able to install it."

As they carried the box and groceries up to her apartment, Maurice worried they hadn't seen the last of Peltier. Was he the danger Schulz had warned them of? Or was Schulz actually the man they should watch out for? There were too many moving parts.

Maurice figured it would be best to be wary of both men until they knew more.

Amelie put Maurice to work opening the box while she put away the groceries and carried the box of condoms into the bedroom. She didn't want to advertise the fact she'd purchased such a big box and appear overly confident he'd stick around to go through all of them. But it didn't hurt to have a supply on hand.

She shook out a few packets and tucked them into the top drawer of her nightstand, right next to the lubrication jelly she kept on hand for when she powered up her battery-operated boyfriend. A thrill of anticipation sent heat throughout her body to pool low in her belly. Maybe they could use one of those packets after installing the surveillance system.

She shoved the box containing the rest of the condoms under her bed. Within easy reach. Who knew? She could be lucky enough to go through the handful she'd dropped inside her nightstand pretty fast, especially if he stole her panties again.

She almost stripped them off again just to tease him. Maybe she could climb the ladder while he braced it at the bottom.

With a sigh, she left her panties on. The bakery might be closed on Monday, but it was on Main Street. They would be hanging the cameras on the exterior of the building. She didn't mind Maurice looking up her skirt to her naked bottom, but she sure as hell didn't want to moon the rest of the town.

They spent the next two hours installing cameras at all four external corners of the building, as well as one in the kitchen, one at the front of her store where the display cases were and another in the living room of her apartment.

Once they were all in place and operational, Amelie connected them to the internet. Following the detailed instructions, she set it up so she could monitor the perimeter of the building from her cell phone or from the desktop computer on the counter at the front of the bakery.

"This is so cool." Amelie paged through the various camera views by swiping her finger across her cell phone screen.

Maurice leaned over her shoulder and pressed a kiss to her cheek. "I'm glad you drew the line at the bedroom."

She laughed. "What? You don't want to make our own X-rated videos?"

"I prefer to *do* rather than just *watch*." He turned her around, pulled her into his arms and held her close enough she could feel the hard evidence of his desire pressing into her belly. He reached into his pocket and held up a foil packet. "I'm a little more prepared than I was last night."

She laughed and took the condom from his fingers and tucked it between her breasts. "Now?"

"Yes, now. I think I've been hard all day, thinking about you and those panties." His hand slid down to the hem of her dress and up underneath, cupping her ass.

She rose on her toes, wrapped her hands around the back of his neck and kissed him, more than ready to take it to the next level and make use of the condom he'd handed her.

Maurice plundered her mouth, sweeping her tongue with his in a long, slow caress that left her knees weak and her breathing labored.

He scooped her legs from under her and started for the bedroom.

Before he reached the door, Amelie's phone pinged.

"That's the sound the surveillance system makes when it detects motion," she said.

"To check it or not to check it," Maurice murmured. "I don't like the question."

A knock sounded on the door of Amelie's apartment.

Maurice froze. "Expecting anyone?"

"God, I hope not." Amelie frowned. "Oh, wait. Luis said he was coming today."

Maurice closed his eyes for a moment.

The knock sounded again.

With a sigh, he set her on her feet. "I'll get it."

Amelie tugged at the hem of her dress and adjusted the straps.

Maurice opened the door.

Luis stood there with a backpack looped over his shoulder. He frowned. "Maurice, hey. I was looking for Amelie."

Amelie stepped forward. "I'm here, Luis."

Luis's brow dipped as he stared at Maurice blocking the door.

Amelie came to stand beside Maurice. "I'm glad you made it. Come in."

Maurice and Amelie stepped back.

Luis entered, eyeing Maurice. "Did I come at a bad time?"

Amelie hid a smile. "No, not at all."

"I didn't call ahead for a hotel or anything since you said I could stay with you." He glanced around the small apartment. "Maybe I should."

"If you don't mind sleeping on the couch, you can stay here," Amelie offered.

Standing behind Luis, Maurice shook his head vehemently.

"I can manage a couch. I got an apartment in New Orleans, but it comes unfurnished. I'll have to work on finding inexpensive furnishings to get me by. Until then, I'll be sleeping on the floor. A couch sounds nice."

Maurice passed Luis on his way to the refrigerator. "How long do you plan on staying here?"

"No more than two nights. I really need to get set up before I start work. I'm not sure how much free time I'll have after that."

"I can ask around and see if anyone has extra furniture they want to donate to your cause." Amelie almost laughed at the scowl on Maurice's face as he snagged a beer from the refrigerator. "Make yourself at home. Are you hungry?"

"I could eat a bite," Luis said. "I spent the day getting all my utilities set up. I didn't stop for lunch."

"We've been busy all day as well. I haven't had time to make anything for dinner. We could go to the Crawdad Hole. They have a grill, or I can call out for pizza."

"Pizza sounds good." Luis dropped his backpack on the floor and flopped onto the couch. "I'm too tired to go out. But if you want to go, bring something back for me."

Amelie met Maurice's gaze. "Pizza sounds good. I'll call in an order. Does everyone like everything on it?"

"No anchovies," Maurice said.

"Ditto," Luis seconded.

Swallowing her disappointment that she wouldn't be using the condom still tucked between her breasts anytime soon, Amelie placed the call to have pizza delivered.

"I brought the photos and the watch with me." Luis dug inside the backpack, pulled out the photos and the watch and handed them to Amelie.

She sat on the couch beside Luis, spread out the photos and laid the watch to the side.

Maurice sat across from them in a lounge chair. He leaned forward, a frown denting his brow.

They stared at the photos in silence. Amelie turned them over and studied the writing on the back.

After a while, Amelie leaned back and sighed. "I'm not seeing anything that would help us."

Luis's brow twisted. "Help us do what?"

Amelie hesitated. They'd learned so much new information since they'd spoken with Luis in New Orleans. She met Maurice's gaze.

He gave a brief nod. "It's up to you."

Amelie made a decision and turned toward Armand's son. "Luis, Fredrick Schulz paid a visit to us yesterday."

Luis's eyebrows rose. "Oh, yeah?"

"Yeah. He asked me the same things he asked you. He wanted to know if Armand had left any artwork, antiquities or journals with me. He went further to say he didn't think your father's death was an accident or heart attack."

Armand's son pushed a hand through his hair. "I had the same feeling. My father was so full of life. I had a hard time believing he was actually dead."

"Schulz thinks someone is after the same information he asked about." She nodded toward Maurice. "Maurice sent the photos to a techno guru he knows and asked him to do a search on a painting in the background of one of your grandparents' photos."

"What painting?" Luis asked.

Amelie pointed to the one where the young Germaine and Celine posed in their Paris living room before the war. "Do you see the painting over the mantel?"

He squinted at the image and nodded.

"Are you familiar with the work of Claude Monet?" she asked.

Luis's brow wrinkled. "We might have covered him in school. Wasn't he the impressionist?"

"Yes," Amelie said. "That painting is one identified as belonging to your grandparents and was recorded as lost during WWII. Your father told me that his parents packed their valuables and fled Paris before the Nazi occupation."

"So?" Luis shrugged. "My father didn't have a Monet at the restaurant, and I never saw anything like that in his apartment. You were there. He didn't have much of anything."

"I know. But he might've known where his parents hid the painting. At least, someone thinks he might have known where it was." She pinched the bridge of her nose as the image of Armand lying on the floor of his beloved kitchen, cold and unmoving, flooded her memory. "Someone willing to kill to find it."

"Wow." Luis sat back and ran a hand through his hair again. "You think the German was looking for that painting?"

"I don't think it, I know it. He admitted that the Monet was what he was looking for. He claims that he searches for missing artwork lost or stolen during the war. When he finds a piece, he works to return it to the rightful owner or to a museum to be appreciated by many."

"And you believe him?" Luis shook his head. "Or is he looking to be the next owner of the recovered painting?"

"We don't know." Amelie stared down at the photos. "If your grandparents hid it, don't you think they would've left their son, your father, some clues as to where to find it?"

"You think the photos or the watch contain the clues?" Luis leaned forward again.

"We hoped," Maurice said.

Luis studied the photos. "I don't see it." His gaze went to the numbers inside the pocket watch. "Unless the numbers are the clue."

Maurice's phone chirped with an incoming call. He glanced down at the screen. "It's Swede. Maybe he's made some progress with the numbers or Schulz." He answered. "Hey, Swede. I'm putting you on speaker." He touched the screen. "Go ahead. Amelie is with me, along with Luis Benoît."

"I found some information about Fredrick Schulz. Apparently, he is what he said he was, a European art historian. His name appears in a few articles discussing the search for and recovery of art stolen or lost during WWII. The articles indicate he didn't keep any of the works for himself but helped to get them back to the families who owned them, or to museums, if there were no descendants to claim them."

"That might only be on the artwork reported in the articles. We don't know if some pieces weren't reported," Maurice said.

"True." Swede went on. "I dug into Schulz's background. He wasn't born Schulz. He changed his last name from Weiss. His grandfather was a guard at Auschwitz from 1942 through 1945. He committed suicide at the end of the war, like so many Nazis did, rather than stand trial for their atrocities. Fredrick's father committed suicide years later after living in the shadow of his father's crimes. Fredrick was raised by his mother, an artist who believed art was for all to see."

"That would explain his desire to recover lost masterpieces," Amelie said.

"Or collect them," Maurice added.

"Either way, I don't know if you should trust him," Swede said. "On a brighter note, I ran those numbers from the pocket watch through several algorithms. Coordinates didn't make sense. I couldn't find any dates that would make sense either. However..." Swede paused. "I ran them through variations of corresponding letters in the alphabet."

"I take it you had some success?" Maurice asked.

"I did," Swede said. "Because Armand and his parents were chefs, I came up with the following— you might want to get a pen and paper."

"Hold on." Amelie jumped up and ran to the counter, where she kept a pen and a pad of paper she used to jot down her grocery lists. She was back in less than two seconds. "Okay."

Swede called out the letters one at a time. "S.O.U.F.F.L.E.A.U.F.R.O.M.A.G.E."

As she wrote the last letter, Amelie's heart skipped a beat. *"Soufflé au Fromage."* She met Luis's gaze.

His eyes widened. "The one dish I could never get right when he was still alive," he said softly. "What does it mean?"

Amelie pressed a hand to her chest. "I think I know."

CHAPTER 11

AMELIE STOOD. "I don't know why I didn't think of it before." She ran to her bedroom, to the only antique she'd kept from her parents' estate, a cabinet they'd called a commode with the door on the front that could be locked with a key. The key had been lost long ago, and the door remained unlocked. She used it to store throw blankets. The drawer above the door opened by pushing in. A spring engaged, and the drawer popped open. She reached inside, pressed a hidden button and a hidden drawer popped out.

Lying in a plastic bag with several silica gel packets was the recipe book that had belonged to Armand and his parents before him.

She pulled it out of the bag, carried it into the

living room and laid it on the table beside the photographs.

Luis ran his hand over the worn leather binding. "Is that my father's recipe book?"

Amelie nodded. "He gave it to me the night before he died and told me to keep it safe. It had all the recipes he and his parents had created through the years."

Luis nodded. "Makes sense that he gave it to you." He glanced up, his lips twisting. "You were his protégé. I was still an angry kid."

"Is there a *Soufflé au Fromage* recipe in that book?" Maurice asked.

Amelie nodded and turned the pages until she reached the *Soufflé au Fromage* recipe she'd made on numerous occasions in Paris.

"Did you find it?" Swede asked, reminding Amelie that he was still on speaker.

"She did," Maurice responded.

Amelie stared at the page, noting the strange use of capital letters in the middle of words or oddly bolded letters throughout the list of ingredients and instructions. She wrote down all the letters and some numbers that stood out on the pad, then sat back.

Maurice came to kneel on the floor beside her. "NTH. That could stand for north."

Amelie underlined the next word. "CLIMB."

Luis ran his finger beneath the next word. "PASS."

"VBWWALL?" Amelie shook her head. "I see WALL, but what does VBW mean?"

Maurice pointed to the next word. "That's FIND."

"US." Amelie underlined the two letters and then the next word. "THERE."

"What I'm hearing are the words north, climb, pass, VBW, wall, find, us, and there," Swede said.

Amelie stared at the words, checked the recipe, and flipped to the next page, where the words didn't have the weird capitalization and bolded letters. "That's it."

"If that's the clue, we're no closer to locating anything," Maurice said.

"Sounds like instructions once you get somewhere," Swede said.

"But where?" Luis asked.

"There has to be another clue to get us wherever *there* is," Maurice said.

"Let me know if you discover anything else," Swede said. "In the meantime, I need to get home to my wife."

"Thanks, Swede," Maurice said. "You've been a big help."

"Wish I could be even more help. We're not there yet," Swede said.

Amelie sighed. "But we're getting closer."

After Swede ended the call, Amelie thumbed through the recipe book but didn't find anything else that jumped out.

When her phone pinged, she looked up. "That's the surveillance system." She reached for her phone and brought up the camera views. "Pizza's here."

Maurice hurried out and down the stairs to collect the pizza.

They spent the next hour eating pizza, drinking beer and going over the words until they agreed to sleep on it and try again in the morning.

Mentally and physically exhausted, Amelie tossed a pillow and a blanket on the couch for Luis. "I'm going to get my shower and go to bed."

"I'm pretty tired myself," Luis said.

"You want to use the bathroom before I tie it up?" she asked.

"Yeah. That beer went right through me." Luis walked through her bedroom into the bathroom and closed the door.

Maurice pulled her into his arms and kissed her briefly. "I can sleep downstairs in the bakery or on the floor in here."

"That's sweet of you," she said. "But no. You're sleeping with me. That is, if you still want to."

"That's a hell yeah." He chuckled and kissed her again. "What about Luis?"

Amelie grimaced. "The walls are thin."

Maurice nodded. "We'll postpone any mattress gymnastics while he's here. But I'd like a raincheck."

"You got it." She cupped his cheek. "You really are special, you know that?"

"I think I'll take that as a compliment." He winked and stepped away as the bathroom door opened and Luis emerged.

"It's all yours," Luis said and flopped on the couch.

"Goodnight, Luis," Amelie said. She grabbed Maurice's hand and dragged him into the room with her, closing the door behind her.

"Think he noticed?" Maurice whispered with a teasing grin.

"Yes, I noticed," Luis called out from the other room. "I'm not a kid. What you do in your own bedroom is not my business. Just keep it down. Some of us don't have a significant other at this time."

Amelie laughed and whispered very softly in Maurice's ear. "The shower will drown out some noise." She reached for the condom between her breasts and held it up. Then she walked backward into the bathroom.

Maurice followed.

AFTER MAKING love in the shower, Maurice spooned Amelie's naked body as she fell asleep. For him, sleep didn't come easily. Breaking the code of the numbers on the watch was just the beginning. Where else would they find the rest of the clues?

They were on the right track. They just didn't know where it was headed.

Armand had left so little behind. Had Luis donated a critical item that contained the rest of the clues leading to the location of the Monet?

Maurice stared up at the ceiling well into the night, making no headway on discovering anything of use or a new angle to pursue.

He must have fallen asleep, because the next thing he knew, Amelie's alarm went off.

She silenced it quickly and started to ease out of the bed.

Maurice's arm tightened around her long enough to steal a kiss.

She sighed and kissed him back. "You're a bad influence," she whispered.

"How so?"

"This is the first time since I opened the bakery that I haven't wanted to get up and go to work."

"Hmmm. I'd say that's the best kind of bad," he said and nuzzled her neck.

"It is." Amelie draped her leg over his and rubbed her sex against his thigh. "How quiet can we be?"

"Instead of hard and fast, we could aim for slow and sensuous," he suggested.

Amelie reached into the nightstand. "I have to be downstairs in fifteen minutes. Let's do this."

Slow and sensuous proved to be as good as hard and fast. It just took a lot more control. But it was worth it.

They were fully dressed and tiptoeing out the door with a minute to spare.

Luis didn't budge from his position sprawled across the couch, sound asleep with his mouth open.

Maurice paused on his way past the coffee table and picked up the watch, the recipe book and the photos. He was convinced they were missing something.

While Amelie was busy baking, he'd give it another shot.

In between helping Amelie move trays of

dough from the refrigerator into the ovens and out of the ovens to cooling racks, Maurice drank coffee and studied the photos, the watch and the recipe book.

Several times, Amelie would stop in passing and look over his shoulder for a few moments before a timer beeped and she was back at it. By the time the freshly baked pastries and bread were glazed, sprinkled and filled with cream, the sun had begun to rise.

Maurice moved the photos from the kitchen to the counter behind the display case and laid the watch beside them.

The watch still showed one o'clock. Maurice snorted. What good was a watch that didn't work? It would only ever be right twice a day.

Amelie passed him on her way to flip the sign on the door from closed to open. She came to stand beside him and looked at the watch.

"Isn't it strange that Armand kept that watch his father gave him for all those years and never got it fixed?" She shook her head. "It's been one o'clock for decades."

"Why wouldn't he get it fixed?"

She shrugged. "Never had the time?"

"The man worked in a restaurant," Maurice pointed out. "Did they serve breakfast?"

Amelie shook her head. "No."

"What time did he go to work?"

"Between nine and ten each day," she said. "It allowed him to sleep in after being up late the night before but gave him enough time to prepare for the lunch crowd."

"Surely, he could've taken the time in the morning to drop the watch off to have it repaired."

"I offered to drop it off for him." Amelie's eyes narrowed. "He said his father had given it to him like that, and he had no intention of changing it."

Maurice studied the watch again, picked it up, turned it over and laid it down next to the photo of Germaine and Celine standing in front of the St. Louis Cathedral with its three steeples and the clock in the middle.

"Holy shit," Maurice said and then laughed out loud. "That's it."

Amelie moved closer and looked down at the photo. "What's it?"

"It was right there all this time, and we just didn't see it."

Amelie's brow puckered. "What didn't we see?"

"Armand refused to fix the watch."

"So?"

"What time is it stuck on?" he asked.

"One o'clock." Amelie looked from the watch

back to the photo. Her eyes widened. "I'll be damned. The clock on the cathedral was photographed at one o'clock." She looked up. "Is that the clue?"

"It has to be," Maurice picked up the photo. "That's the *where* we were looking for. Don't you see? Either the painting is hidden in the cathedral, or it's where we'll find another clue. We need to get to New Orleans."

"I can't leave the bakery. Not now." She nodded toward the vehicle pulling into the parking space out front. "I have customers. Besides, the cathedral doesn't open this early."

Maurice pulled out his phone and looked up the St. Louis Cathedral's hours of operation. "It opens at nine o'clock. If you can't get away, I could have one of the guys come here to take over your protection while I run to New Orleans to see if I can find the location indicated in the clue."

Amelie's jaw hardened. "You cannot go on this treasure hunt without me. Germaine and Celine might've set up the initial clues, but if what you find is another clue, it might be of Armand's doing. I knew Armand better than anyone, even his son. I'm going. That's non-negotiable."

Maurice pulled her into his arms for a quick

kiss. "Agreed. Besides, I don't like the idea of someone else in charge of your safety."

She raised an eyebrow. "Even one of your own teammates?"

"I trust them with my life. I just don't know if I could step away as your protector. Not yet. Not until we remove the danger in this situation."

"Good. I don't want any other protector but you. And I don't want to be left behind. Now that we've got that settled, I'm going with you," Amelie said. "You realize St. Louis Cathedral is a national park, don't you?

Maurice nodded. "It was part of the Louisiana Purchase."

"If, in the process of retrieving the painting or another clue, we do anything to damage the structure, it's considered a federal crime. Depending on the extent of the damage, it could be considered a misdemeanor or even a felony.

"Then we'll do our best not to damage it or get caught."

"I'd feel better if we had a plan before we rush off to New Orleans. I want to understand the other clues better so we're not blindly poking around a national park. But first, I have to take care of my business."

"Fair enough. We'll work through the morning

rush. But see if you can get someone to fill in for you as soon as possible. Once we leave here, I'd like to swing by the boat factory. I can arrange to have Remy and some of the other Brotherhood Protectors there to help brainstorm the possible meanings of the clues. I'll also get Swede working on obtaining blueprints of the cathedral if they're anywhere to be found."

A smile spread across Amelie's face. "Now, that's a plan I can get behind. If there's one thing that makes me crazy, it's going off half-cocked."

"Then we'll go fully cocked."

The door opened, and the first customers of the day entered—a young mother and her three-year-old daughter.

The rush proved heavy and steady all the way to ten thirty when they finally caught a break. Amelie had texted Gisele, who offered to have her assistant, Lena Drummond, man the bakery for the rest of the day as soon as she showed up at the Mamba Wamba Gift Shop.

Amelie would need to stick around long enough to show Lena the ropes, how to run the point-of-sale system and anything else she needed to know to keep the business running in Amelie's absence.

Luis came down at nine-thirty. While he ate one of Amelie's amazing eclairs, they filled him in on what they'd found.

"I'm going with you," Luis said.

"If the directions are leading us to one of the bell towers, we might have a problem," Maurice said. "The bell towers are off-limits to the public. We'd have to sneak in. That might be considered a crime."

"I'm willing to risk it," Luis said.

"A federal crime," Amelie clarified. "It would show up on your record and could keep you from getting a job or cause you to lose the one you have yet to start."

"Then we'll have to make sure we don't get caught," Luis said.

Maurice grinned. "I like the way he thinks."

Amelie shook her head. "You two are impossible."

"And you like to follow the rules," Luis said. "Remember what my father always told you?"

Amelie nodded, "Don't try to go exactly by the recipe."

"Or rules," Luis interjected. "Go on."

"Sometimes, you have to go with your gut." She sighed. "I miss him."

Luis gave her a half-smile. "Me, too."

"It would've been a lot simpler to find the painting if he hadn't died," Amelie said softly.

"And told us what all this means and where to look without having to unravel the clues," Luis muttered.

Amelie stood as one of the local moms entered the bakery and asked for two dozen cookies to take to her child's school for an afternoon snack.

Halfway through the morning, Lena appeared in the doorway, wearing jeans, a Nirvana T-shirt and black army boots. She carried a backpack slung over her shoulder. "Hey, Amelie. Gisele said you needed someone to cover for you while you run off to New Orleans for the rest of the day."

"That's right. Thanks for coming on such short notice."

"No worries," Lena said. "One thing, though. I have a test in Calculus tomorrow. If things get slow around here, do you mind if I use the time to study?"

"Not at all," Amelie said. "I'm just glad you're able to fill in for me. You can drop your backpack behind the counter, then follow me."

Maurice admired how quickly and efficiently Amelie brought Lena up to speed and let her handle several customers before she deemed her ready to conquer the world. Or, at least, the bakery.

She drove the bakery van with Maurice and Luis as passengers to the boarding house, where they picked up Maurice's pickup and left the van parked out front.

Next stop was the old boat factory, where a few of his teammates would be waiting to help them go over the clues.

Maurice led Amelie, followed by Luis, through the active boat factory, filled with sheets of aluminum, the machines needed to bend and form the aluminum and more. At the far end of the factory floor stood a door leading into the remodeled section of the building, outfitted as a war room with a conference table, a bank of computers with an array of monitors and a large screen at the end of the table.

As soon as they walked in, Remy, Gerard, Lucas, Beau and Xavier, pushed to their feet.

Remy was the first to approach Amelie and Luis. "Welcome to the headquarters of the Bayou Brotherhood Protectors." He held out his hand to Luis. "I'm Remy Montagne, lead over this branch of the Brotherhood Protectors."

Luis shook Remy's hand as he glanced around the room. "This is amazing. And the boat factory is beyond cool."

Remy waved a hand toward the conference table. "I know you want to get to New Orleans early enough to give yourself time to follow the clues. If you'll take a seat, we can get started. Swede, bring up what you all discovered in the recipe book, using the numeric positioning of the alphabet."

The string of words appeared on the big screen.

CLIMB PASS TIME EGLW WALL FIND US THERE

"ACCORDING TO LUIS," Swede continued, "the pocket watch Armand Benoît gave him prior to his death hasn't worked for as long as he remembers." The photo of the watch appeared on the screen with the other clues. "The hands on the watch are frozen in the one o'clock position, which corresponds to the photograph of Germaine and Celine Benoît standing in front of the St. Louis Cathedral at exactly one o'clock. This leads us to believe the missing Monet painting could be hidden inside the cathedral.

"Now that you know the location is the St. Louis Cathedral," Swede said, "let's see how these words might apply." He added a photograph of the cathedral to the display. "As you can see, St. Louis Cathedral has three towers, with a clock mounted in the center. The center tower also contains the bells."

Maurice moved closer to the end of the conference table to point at the central tower. "The first word we identified was CLIMB," he stated. "Since the clock in the photo matches the time on the pocket watch, we think it means the clock tower of the cathedral is where we'd climb."

"PASS is next, then TIME," Maurice said. "We figure you'll have to climb past the clock."

"The next letters are where we have to get creative," Remy said. "EGLW WALL. Does that mean you need to pass EGLW WALL or pass EGLW, then go to a wall? And which wall?"

"What is EGLW?" Gerard asked.

"That has us stumped," Maurice said.

"What if we take each letter separately?" Remy suggested. "What object in the St. Louis Cathedral starts with an E and can be found in the central tower?"

Silence stretched.

Maurice shook his head. "If the first word is climb and you pass the clock, what would come next?"

"The bells," Amelie said.

"Bells' notes start with B, not E," Remy pointed out.

"Unless the bells have names," Maurice said. "Swede?"

"They do," Swede came back. "The largest one is the Victoire, and there's one called the Philomena Virginia."

"Again, not E," Remy said.

"Okay, so we don't know what EGLW stands for. We can figure it out when we get there. How many places above the clock would be big enough to hide a painting anyway? We'll need to check all the walls after we pass the clock. It has to be there."

"FIND US THERE, has to mean the spot where the painting is hidden," Amelie said. "Why does it say US, as in more than one?"

"They escaped with valuables. Maybe they hid more than just the painting," Maurice suggested." He looked around the room, his gaze stopping at Amelie. "We don't have all the answers, but we have enough to focus on the central tower of the cathedral above the clock."

"It'll have to be enough." Amelie's lips tightened in a straight line. "We have to make it work because we might not get more than one shot at sneaking in."

"Before we go to jail or are fined and banned from ever visiting the cathedral again," Maurice said.

"Or any other national park," Luis added.

"Maurice, are you suggesting you and Amelie will attempt the climb?" Remy asked.

Luis raised a hand. "And me."

"Don't you think we should send in a subset of our team?" Remy said. "We're trained combatants. If Armand Benoît was murdered, whoever killed him might be waiting to claim the prize and might kill again to get it."

Amelie shot a glance toward Maurice. "Armand entrusted the watch and recipe book to Luis and me. He wanted us to follow the clues. If there's something to be found, it should be us finding it."

Remy's gaze shot to Maurice.

"It wouldn't hurt to have backup," Maurice compromised.

"We're supposed to do everything in our power to protect our clients," Remy reminded him.

Maurice's jaw tightened. "And I will do everything in my power to protect Amelie."

"Me, too," Luis said.

Maurice nodded. "I doubt we can sneak an entire team into the tower. But if we're going in with three, we might as well take four. Do you have someone in mind?"

Remy nodded. "Me."

"You're the boss," Xavier noted. "Shouldn't you be directing the rest of us? I'll be the fourth on the infil team."

Remy frowned. "Maurice? Xavier is an experienced—"

"Navy SEAL." Maurice gave the man a chin lift. "We never worked together on active duty, but I know his record. Yes. I'd take him in a heartbeat."

Remy turned to the others. "The rest of us will set up a perimeter around the cathedral, arriving at different times."

"Swede, we'll need pictures of the German, Fredrick Schulz, and the Frenchman, Eugene Peltier, who claims to be a cultural preservationist, and whatever you can dig up on him. Could you get it to us ASAP?"

"On it," Swede said.

"When do we leave?" Remy asked.

"Immediately," Amelie said, "if not sooner."

Maurice nodded. "We don't know if Schulz or Peltier was responsible for the death of Amand

Benoît or someone entirely different. But they were able to find Bayou Mambaloa. I say we locate the Monet and get it into the right hands before Armand's killer turns his sights on Luis and Amelie." He lifted his chin. "We leave as soon as we gear up."

CHAPTER 12

AMELIE WAS SHOCKED at the amount of equipment, arms and protective gear the Brotherhood Protectors had in the room they called the arsenal. "You could wage your own war with the stuff you have here."

"That's not our purpose." Maurice helped sift through a drawer of lethal-looking knives and pulled out one that appeared to be plastic. He found a sheath for it and held it up. "It's better to have it and not need it than to need it and not have it."

She raised an eyebrow. "You're taking a toy knife into a gunfight?"

"It won't be a gunfight. Guests at the cathedral have to pass through a metal detector to get inside.

Otherwise, I'd load you up with body armor, a helmet and bubble wrap."

"Nothing says love like the gift of body armor and bubble wrap." She ran her fingers up his chest. "You like me better alive, I take it."

"Much better." He strapped the knife scabbard to her wrist and pulled the long sleeve of her T-shirt over it.

He reached back into the drawer of knives and found a thin set of three with a scabbard and strapped it to his forearm. Moving to another drawer, he extracted several long zip ties, folded them and tucked them into his pocket. In yet another drawer, he selected a small plastic file and slid it in with the three knives.

He grabbed a mini can of mace and tossed it to Amelie. "Careful where you aim that mace."

She tucked it into her jeans pocket.

"Do I get to carry a gun?" Luis asked as he inspected the racks of weapons, including AR-15s, mini machine guns and handguns of all shapes and sizes.

"Have you ever fired one?" Maurice asked.

"No," Luis admitted. "Although I'm sure I could figure it out. How hard could it be? You point and pull the trigger."

"No guns for him," Amelie said.

"My thoughts, exactly," Maurice said with a grimace. "Tell you what, Luis, when this blows over, I'll take you out for target practice. If you like it, we'll get you signed up for firearms training and a safety class."

"I'd love that, but I'll have to wait until I have a better handle on my work schedule."

"The offer is open," Maurice said, handing Luis earbuds. "This is your communication device that'll keep you in contact with the team. Keep chatter to a minimum."

"Yes, sir." Luis fit the communication device into his ear. "Testing. Testing. Can you hear me?"

Maurie pressed a hand to his ear. "Very loud and clear." He handed a set to Amelie.

She placed them in her ears. With a wink, she flipped her hair. "Hey sexy, can you hear me?"

"Affirmative," he said. "Along with everyone else on this frequency.

"Really?" she squeaked.

"You bet," Remy said.

"You can talk sexy to me anytime, as long as my wife, the senator's daughter, approves." Beau chuckled. "Coming over to the dark side, are you?"

"If wearing body armor and breaking into

church towers counts," Amelie lifted her shoulders and let them fall, "I guess I am."

The rest of the team performed a comm check, verifying all radios were sending and receiving.

"We'll take my truck into New Orleans," Maurice said.

"Luis and I will take my SUV," Xavier said. "That way, we arrive separately. And since we've purchased our entrance tickets online, we don't have to stand in line."

Maurice drew a deep breath. "We'll converge inside at the base of the clock tower."

"The rest of us will arrive in my SUV," Remy said. "We'll park in a parking garage, split up and take point around the exterior of the building. We'll be there if you need us."

Maurice checked his watch. "Takes a little over an hour to get to New Orleans and park. That will leave us two hours inside the cathedral. Hopefully, it won't take that long to find what we're looking for."

"Everyone ready?" Remy asked.

His team, Luis and Amelie all nodded as one.

"Let's go!"

They filed out of the boat factory, loaded into vehicles and left, taking different routes through town before they headed southeast into New Orleans.

Amelie sat quietly in the passenger seat, wondering what they'd find and if they'd meet any resistance from the National Park Service or people interested in owning the long-lost Monet.

"Worried?" Maurice asked.

She nodded. "A little. I'm more anxious than anything to see how this treasure hunt works out."

He reached across the console for her hand. "Promise you'll stay close to me. I can't protect you if you're more than three feet away."

She nodded. "Three feet or less." She squeezed his hand. "I feel safe when I'm with you."

He chuckled. "I feel all kinds of crazy when I'm with you."

"Is that a bad thing?" she asked.

"It's a I've-never-felt-more-alive thing." He glanced toward her. "Like the sun finally came out."

She smiled. "I like having you around."

He arched an eyebrow. "Just to make you feel safe?"

"And so much more," she said softly. "I've spent most of my adult life working toward a goal, a career, a business and haven't taken the time to work on me." She smiled at the road ahead. "You showed me what I was missing. Now that I know what it is, I can work on that."

"And what was it you were missing?"

"Like you, I was missing someone who makes me feel alive. In my case, I wasn't necessarily in a black fog of grief, but I was in a tunnel headed for my career goals, never looking left or right at the things that could make me happy along the way." She drew in a breath and let it out. "Now, I understand the saying that it's not the destination or the journey that makes life great. It's the people." She looked down at the scarred hand she was holding. "Thank you."

All too soon, they entered New Orleans and navigated the busy streets, arriving at a parking garage close enough to walk to Jackson Square to reach their goal of the St. Louis Cathedral.

Amelie's stomach churned as she pushed the truck door open.

Maurice appeared in front of her, placed his hands on her waist and lowered her to the ground in a slow slide down his body.

Her stomach churned in an entirely different way as her feet touched the ground.

Ever so gently, Maurice brushed a kiss across her forehead and whispered so softly she couldn't be sure of the words. She thought they sounded like, *Be careful, my love.*

How could that be? He couldn't commit. His love had died in his arms. He wasn't ready to move on to anything more than casual sex.

Casual, mind-blowing, don't-stop-now loving she didn't want to live without but might have to when he sank back down in the black hell of survivor's guilt.

She lifted her face and caught his lips with hers in a brief kiss. "Promise me something?"

He tucked a strand of her hair behind her ear. "Promise what?"

"That when this is all over, you'll forgive yourself for being alive and get on with the job of living."

His lips tipped upward. "Every minute I spend with you, I get a little closer."

"And if I'm not with you anymore? Will you still feel the same? Will you be done with oppressive sorrow? Ready to embrace happiness, however it best manifests for you.

Maurice's eyes narrowed, and his brow formed a deep V. "You're going to be okay. We'll get through this."

"Yeah. Of course. I just want to know *you'll* be okay if we go our separate ways." *Because I won't be.*

She bit down on her tongue to keep from blurting it out.

"What are you talking about? We're not done, are we?" A ruddy red stained his cheeks. "If that's how you feel, you picked a helluva a time to tell me."

Amelie shook her head. "No, not at all. I just know this whole thing we've had was built on air. No commitment. I've seen you smile and laugh over the past few days. I care about you and want you to be happy with or without me."

He stared hard into her eyes. Then he crushed her to his chest and claimed her mouth in a searing kiss that burned all the way through to her heart.

The earbuds in Amelie's ears crackled. "X and K heading in. Here's to breaking rules. See you on the wrong side."

"We're not done," Maurice said, the fierceness fading into tenderness. He brushed his injured hand along the curve of her jaw. Once more, he gathered her close, this time gently and touched his lips to hers. "Not done."

He took her hand in his and led her across Jackson Square to the entrance of St. Louis Cathedral, where he held up his cell phone to show the online entry tickets for both of them. After the gate guard scanned their QR codes, they passed through the metal detector without setting it off.

Inside the cathedral, Maurice touched a hand to Amelie's back and guided her into the beautiful cathedral, aiming for the central clock and bell tower.

"M and A are in the building," Maurice said softly, his voice filling Amelie's ear.

"We've got your six," Remy's voice came through. "Go get it."

This was it. The chance to bring the work of a master back into the light. A thrill of anticipation rippled through Amelie as she strode alongside Maurice through the cavernous cathedral.

Along the way, Amelie forced a smile and pretended to admire paintings, stained glass and the beauty of the architecture around her. Any other time, she wouldn't have to fake it.

Now that she was on the trail of a lost treasure that might or might not be hidden in the clock tower, she pushed her personal worries to the back burner and forged ahead.

Bells rang, announcing the quarter hour. The sound echoed long after the bells stopped ringing.

"Fifteen minutes until they ring again," Maurice noted.

They wouldn't want to be in the bell tower

when the next bells tolled. The sound would be deafening.

They came to a door tucked into a shadowy corner. The sign posted on the panel read AUTHORIZED PERSONNEL ONLY.

Amelie reached for the knob as Maurice automatically reached for the file in the knife scabbard.

Expecting the door to be locked, Amelie was surprised when the knob turned freely. She pulled the door open and looked at Maurice.

He stepped around her and took point, trading the file for one of the knives, arming himself in case they ran into trouble.

The first set of steps was wide and polished, leading to a landing, a turn and more steps, then another landing, another turn and more steps, before continuing upward to the floor with the clock overlooking Jackson Square.

"PASS TIME," Amelie murmured as they rose above the clock.

The stairs narrowed, curving upward, forcing them to ascend single file. Maurice, still in the lead, climbed steadily upward. They passed four smaller bells, two above them, and finally reached the largest bell that hung over the others. Light shining through a round window illuminated a beam with the image of an eagle burned into the wood. Beneath it was the year 1949.

Amelie stretched her arm out and ran her fingers across the image of the eagle. "EGL. Eagle."

"Damned door's locked. Working it." Xavier's voice startled Amelie in the silence of the bell tower.

She turned on the staircase. With the bells taking up the center of the tower, there was no floor, only beams crisscrossing the space. Some held the weight of the bells beneath them. Others carried the weight of the roof above.

"EGL for eagle, but why the W?" Amelie whispered in deference to the sanctity of the cathedral and the bells. "And which WALL?"

"The W might not be part of EGL. It could be telling us which wall," Maurice said. "West."

He turned in that direction and studied the wall accessible only by the beam leading to it.

"Stay here," Maurice said, and then stepped off the stairs onto the beam suspended in the air over the layers of bells below. Placing one foot in front of the other on a joist narrower than a gymnast's balance beam, Maurice spread his arms wide. One false step or stumble, and he could fall all twenty or more feet to the nearest floor located at the clock level. Add the probability of slamming into bells and beams along the way, and the ultimate landing wouldn't be pretty.

Amelie's gut clenched the further he moved away from her. She couldn't reach out and steady him. All she could do was hold her breath until he reached the west wall.

"FIND US THERE," she said, her voice shaking with anxiety.

Maurice finally reached the wall and braced his hands against it. For a long moment, he studied a section of wood paneling.

"What do you see?" Amelie asked.

"Initials carved into a single panel." He pulled his cell phone from his pocket and shined a light at the wall. "G + C."

Amelie's heart fluttered, and her pulse picked up, racing so fast her head spun. "Find us here. You found them. Germaine and Celine. You found the spot."

Maurice felt along the seam between the wood panels, tugged, pushed and frowned. "If this is the place, all they left were their initials." He looked over his shoulder at Amelie. "Any ideas?"

"Maybe it's not just the single panel that moves." Amelie itched to be there next to him, working with him to figure out how to get behind the panel.

He tried pulling a corner at a time, then pushing. When he leaned into the bottom corner, the panel shifted slightly. Applying more pressure, the bottom leaned in, and the top of the panel tipped outward, toward him.

Maurice shined his light into the space created. Then he reached down and dragged out what appeared to be a leatherbound map case with a strap. Without turning, he held it in the air.

Steps sounded on the spiral staircase.

"He found it," Amelie called out, her gaze on Maurice and the map case. She couldn't wait to see the Monet, a painting that had been lost for decades.

Maurice slid the strap over his shoulder and turned slowly on the beam. When he glanced up briefly, his eyes widened. "Amelie!"

Amelie spun on the narrow step. Four steps below her, two men wearing black face masks and baseball caps appeared around the curve of the spiral staircase. The one in the lead held a pistol in his hand. "Don't move," he said, "or I'll shoot you, then I'll shoot him."

Amelie raised her hands. She couldn't step to the side to place herself between the gunman and Maurice.

The man with the gun waved it toward

Maurice. "Toss the case to your girlfriend. Make it good. If she misses or drops it, I'll shoot you, then I'll shoot her."

Maurice slipped the strap off his shoulder. "If the case falls, it could shatter and destroy what's inside."

"Then you better hope she catches it." He jerked the gun. "Do it. I don't have all day."

"I don't know," she said, making her voice shake. That part wasn't hard as her entire body was shaking. "I don't think I can catch it. What if it knocks me over? It'll fall all the way to the bottom. We can't let that happen."

"Then catch it," the gunman gritted out.

"You need someone with bigger hands," she said. "Do you know what's inside? Do you have any idea how much money is at stake?"

The guy behind the gunman nudged him. "Ask her."

"Shut up," the gunman hissed.

The guy behind him leaned around his partner. "How much?"

"Hundreds of thousands. Maybe four-hundred-thousand or more."

"What's so special that it's worth that much?" the guy behind the gunman asked.

"Shut the fuck up, asshole. We're getting paid to

get it and get out." He focused on Maurice again. "Throw it now."

"Please," Amelie begged. "It's a famous painting by one of the greatest artists of all time. I'd rather you took it than have it be destroyed."

"I'll catch it," the masked man in the back pushed past the gunman and came to stand two steps down from her. "Okay, throw it."

Amelie, her hands still in the air, glanced at the watch on her wrist. Any second now, the bells would ring, giving her the distraction she needed.

"Go ahead and throw it," she yelled to Maurice. "He's going to catch it."

Maurice's eye narrowed.

"Do you want him to shoot me?" she demanded. "Throw it. Now!"

Maurice bunched his muscles, bent and thrust the map case into the air.

Bong! Bong! Bong!

While the man's attention was on the map case, his hands reaching into the air, Amelie slammed her foot as hard as she could into the man's shoulder, sending him flying down the spiral staircase into his partner.

Amelie immediately pivoted, flung her hand in the air and snagged the strap in the crook of her arm. The weight of the case, plus its momentum, pulled it down. The strap on her arm arrested its downward trajectory so fast it snapped back and hit her in the face.

She slammed into the stair rail, hitting it low on her hip.

With both hands in the air, she had no way to steady herself and regain her balance. The heavy map case pulled her over the rail.

CHAPTER 13

MAURICE COULD TELL Amelie was revving up to do something when she yelled at him to throw the map case. From where he was standing, he could do nothing to help her. He figured once the map case left his hands, they'd shoot him.

What could one lone female do against two men, one of whom was pointing a loaded gun at her? She was going to get herself shot.

"Don't do it," he muttered as he cocked his arm. "Don't do it." However, as soon as he thrust the map case into the air, she did it.

Amelie kicked the guy reaching for the case so hard, he flew down the staircase, bulldozing the guy with the gun and sending him tumbling further. The gun flew into the air and fell, bouncing off the big bell on its way to the floor twenty feet below. All of this happened so fast that he didn't know which way to look.

At the same time, the bells started ringing so loudly they reverberated off his eardrums.

In a flash of movement, Amelie turned, flung her hands in the air and caught the map case strap on her arm.

Just when Maurice thought she was safe, the map case bounced back, hitting her in the face, and she lost her balance and tipped over the rail.

"No!" Maurice didn't hesitate, didn't think. He ran across the beam and threw himself downward to the next lower beam. He reached his arms out and caught himself on the wooden joist, hitting it so hard that it knocked the air from his lungs and shot paint through his arms and chest.

He pulled himself up to straddle the brace and searched the floor far below for Amelie's broken body, expecting the worst but praying for a miracle.

The crisscrossing beams, bells and cobwebs made it difficult to see the floor so far below. Where was she? His gut clenched.

If she died...

His pulse pounded hard through his veins like a bass drum against his ears. He couldn't catch his breath.

"Not again," he wheezed through constricted lungs. The scent of garlic and burning flesh filled his memories. His head spun, and his stomach roiled.

No. He couldn't lose it.

Fuck no.

He couldn't see her on the floor below, because she hadn't fallen that far.

Forcing back the dizziness and muscling air back into his lungs, he pushed to his knees and shimmied across the beam, searching, scanning. She had to be close. She had to be alive.

He refused to accept any other option.

A moan sounded directly below him.

He flattened himself to the beam and leaned over.

Amelie lay sprawled across a wider junction of joists, face down...and moving.

"Amelie!" Maurice called out. "Amelie, sweetheart. Answer me."

"Ugh," she groaned.

"Babe, are you hurt?" He snorted. "Of course, you're hurt. Can you tell if anything is broken? Can you move your fingers and toes?"

"I... can...move." To prove it, she pushed her body up on her arms and cursed. "Please tell me you got the number of the truck that ran me over."

"Don't move," Maurice called out.

"Couldn't if I wanted to. Got nowhere to go." She raised her arm. "Didn't drop it. All I got to say is that Monet better be in here." She lay back down on the junction.

"Amelie, talk to me," Maurice said as he looked for a better way to get down. Unfortunately, from where he stood, there wasn't much of a choice other than jumping. At least the beams Amelie was on came close to the spiral staircase.

He glanced up at the tangle of arms and legs that was the pair of thugs who had threatened to shoot them. One appeared unconscious, trapping the other beneath him.

Maurice wasn't sure how long the two would remain incapacitated. He had to get to Amelie and get her down from the tower before they came after them.

And where the hell were Luis and Xavier? They were supposed to have their six. Communications were nil after he'd lost his earbuds in the fall. He suspected Amelie's had been dislodged as well.

Moving further down the beam, away from where Amelie lay, he found a cross piece that was only four feet down, versus the eight feet he'd dropped the first time.

Maurice channeled his inner BUD/S trainee,

the one conditioned to embrace cold and pain, and focused, steadied and dropped onto the post below. He ran to where one beam crossed the one Amelie was on.

This time, he lay on the post, swung his legs over the side and eased himself down until his feet touched a hard surface.

As soon as he was steady, he hurried to Amelie and dropped down in front of her. "Hey. No sleeping on the job."

"Not sleeping," she muttered. "Contemplating."

"Contemplating what?" he asked, glancing around, worried he was taking too long.

"Contemplating my life choices," she said.

"Sweetheart, we need to get you up and out of here before Tweedle Dee and Dumber manage to untangle themselves from the staircase. Let me help you up."

She waved her hand. "I've got this."

He waited.

"Okay, I don't have this. I could use a hand."

He slid a hand beneath her arm and rose, pulling her up with him and bracing himself in case she passed out.

Once she was upright, she swayed, and her eyes rolled back.

Maurice shifted for a better grip.

Then her head came up, she blinked and smiled at him. "Thought I was going to go down, didn't you?" She laughed and coughed, pressing a hand to her chest. "Psych."

"Out of all the starving comedians, I get stuck with you." He slipped the map case off her arm and slung it over his head and across his chest. Then he turned her to face the staircase. "I need you to walk the plank."

"Aye, aye, matey." She placed one foot in front of the other.

He walked her forward, holding her by the hips to correct her balance along the way. They made better progress than he'd expected, crossing over to the spiral staircase without falling to their deaths.

Groans and curses sounded from above.

"I believe Dee and Dumber are on the move. Let me go down first." He stepped in front of Amelie.

Amelie laid a hand on his shoulder. "I'm feeling a little steadier," she said. "Let's get the hell out of here."

Moving as fast as he could without leaving her behind, Maurice hurried down the spiral stairs until they arrived on the floor with the clock.

Maurice glanced around. The gun had fallen to

this level. The last thing he wanted was for the two miscreants, now pounding their way down the stairs, to retrieve the gun and come after them. The pounding sounds increased, even louder than he thought two men could possibly create.

He almost gave up looking for the gun when something shiny caught his attention. "Hold on."

Maurice sprinted across the floor and grabbed the gun.

"Maurice!" Amelie yelled.

On instinct, Maurice spun and dropped low, his heart sinking to the pit of his belly.

Eugene Peltier stood between Maurice and the staircase leading down from the clock tower. He held the woman Maurice loved captive, an arm wrapped around her middle with a gun pressed to her temple. "I will take the case," he said, his tone as cold as his eyes.

"Let her go, and you can have it," Maurice said.

"No. The pretty chef is my insurance policy. I will have the case and the chef until I am clear of American airspace."

Maurice shook his head. "Not an option." You're not taking her anywhere." He pulled the map case over his head with his right hand, while aiming for Peltier's chest with the gun he held with his left hand. "You see, if you shoot her, you lose your leverage and your body shield. You won't have time to shoot another round before I put a bullet in you. It's a lose-lose situation."

Peltier pressed the barrel of the gun harder against Amelie's temple. "Are you willing to stake her life on it? I have nothing to lose," Peltier said. "I wasted two years chasing clues, looking for *The Lady by the Stream*. Two years, following a long list of false clues that lying bastard Benoît gave me when I threatened to kill him. He finally gave them to me, but I killed him anyway. You know where his clues led me? To a cave in Portugal. In it, I found a painting. A picture a child could have painted, titled *Deception*. The bastard deserved to die. He knew where she was all along but kept her hidden away."

Heavy footsteps clomped down the spiral staircase, nearing the bottom. It was only moments before the goons joined the fun.

"Now, I will have the last laugh and the Monet my family was promised for helping the Nazis assimilate into France. A painting my grandfather gave his life for. It will be mine."

Amelie's eyes narrowed.

Maurice was beginning to know that look. Once again, she was revving up to do something.

She mouthed the words, *Shoot him.* Her hand at her side displayed three fingers, then two.

He braced himself, his finger caressing the trigger. "I almost feel sorry for you. Your obsession has consumed your humanity."

One.

Amelie went limp and slipped through Peltier's grip, dropping to the floor.

Maurice fired.

The bullet hit the man in his left shoulder, but he barely jerked backward. Seconds later, he had his gun aimed at Maurice.

Maurice fired again.

Peltier staggered and fired, the bullet going wide.

The two men reached the bottom of the spiral staircase.

Peltier cried out, "Kill him!"

The men rushed Maurice.

He raised the gun and tried to pull the trigger. It misfired. He flung it to the ground, pulled a knife from the scabbard on his arm and flung it at the closest of the two, the blade piercing his neck. The man slowed, clasping a hand to his throat while blood streamed down his arm.

The other guy charged at Maurice like an angry bull.

Maurice waited until the last moment and stepped aside. As the attacker staggered past him, Maurice planted his hand in the middle of the man's back and pushed hard.

He fell, crashing hard against the floor.

"Oh, no, you don't," Amelie said.

Maurice glanced up to find Peltier with his hand fisted in her hair.

"Let go of my hair and I'll let you keep them," she said through clenched teeth.

Maurice followed her hand to where she had it pressed against Peltier's balls with the plastic knife he'd insisted she bring to the party.

"I'm a chef," she said. "I'm pretty good with a knife, and I know how to cut meat."

"Amelie?" Maurice started toward her. "Need a hand?"

"I've got this bastard. You heard him. He killed Armand. He deserves to die." She bared her teeth at him. "Go ahead. Make your move. I don't really need an excuse to bury this knife in you."

Unarmed and bleeding profusely, Peltier wouldn't be a problem for Amelie.

Still, Maurice moved closer, ready to take him out if he tried anything more than pulling her hair. Already, he was losing his grip and swaying. Blood loss did that to a man.

Footsteps pounded on the stairs coming up from below.

Xavier, Luis, Remy, Gerard, Lucas and Beau burst onto the scene. A few steps behind them, huffing and puffing, came Fredrick Schulz.

"Right." Maurice crossed his arms over his chest. "Now you show up."

"Had a little difficulty with the door. It was blocked," Xavier said.

Luis tipped his head toward the German. "Schulz found us another way in."

Remy tipped his head toward Amelie and Peltier. "That woman has rage."

"Tell me about it." Maurice shook his head. "I should be all right with her. I think she might love me."

Amelie shot a glance his way, eyes wide.

Maurice smiled. "And it's a good thing, because I love her right back."

Her lips spread in a radiant smile, which was a little unnerving considering she still had her knife all up in Peltier's business.

Remy elbowed Maurice. "Just remember not to piss her off."

"Roger that," Maurice said.

Remy strode over to Amelie. "Let me take over from here. The police are on their way."

"He killed Armand," she said, her eyes filling.

Maurice moved up behind her. "Yeah. But now you know, and he'll pay. No use ruining your life by taking his."

She lowered her arm and let Remy lead the man away.

Maurice turned her toward him and pulled her into his arms.

She pressed her forehead against his chest. "I heard what you said." She leaned her head back and met his gaze with a watery one of her own. "Did you mean it?" A tear slid down her cheek. "You don't have to, if you don't want to. You know...love me."

He touched a finger to her lips. "I don't say things I don't mean."

Another tear slipped down her cheek. "I'm glad," she said and pressed her forehead against his chest again. "I really didn't know how to compete with a ghost."

He tipped her chin up. "You're not competing with a ghost."

She nodded. "I know that now. I would never want you to forget her or the love you felt for her. That love is a part of you. It made you who you are today. And I'm falling hopelessly in love with you.

So, don't screw it up," she said with a saucy tilt of her head. "I'm wicked with a knife."

"I'll never sleep again at night," he said.

"There are many better things to do at night than sleep," she whispered.

"I can think of quite a few," he said, nuzzling her neck.

"Jesus, Mo," Xavier said. "Get a room."

EPILOGUE

Xavier wandered along Main Street, admiring the way the town had gone all out, stringing lights and hanging colorful banners everywhere for the Annual Frog Leg Festival.

Zydeco music blasted from the pavilion on the square; all the locals were out in force, and a couple thousand tourists had joined them, coming from all over the country to join the fun.

He'd been in Bayou Mambaloa for almost two years. It should be home to him. He should be happy, not dragging his ass through town, wondering if he'd made the right decision to join the Bayou Brotherhood Protectors instead of picking one of the other more exotic locations like Colorado, Montana or Hawaii.

No, he'd decided to return to his home state of Louisiana. He'd been homesick for the food and music and the sense of family he hadn't quite found anywhere else in the world.

And he'd been to a lot of places he'd never heard of. Life as a Navy SEAL hadn't been boring. Always away from his duty station. Deploying with little notice. Never knowing when he'd be back. He'd never been bored.

However, he'd never found a woman who could handle that lifestyle. Or maybe he hadn't wanted to subject a woman to the loneliness she'd endure while he was away. He understood why his buddy's wives had affairs or left them while they were deployed. How could they have a lasting relationship when they were never together?

He sighed. Well, he'd give up the excitement and danger of an active-duty Navy career, purposefully choosing a relaxed and happily boring life in the Louisiana bayous.

Yeah, he'd gotten just what he'd wanted. He should be happy.

Maurice and Amelie emerged from the back of the bakery where they lived in the upstairs apartment. They were blissfully happy, newly engaged, and made Xavier want to puke every time he was around them with all their kissing, touching and loving.

He pretended he hadn't seen them and walked on by.

"Xavier, hold up," Maurice called out.

Caught, he braced himself for the bliss that oozed out of every one of his teammates' pores.

Maurice clapped a hand on Xavier's back. "Dude. You don't look very happy. What's got you down?"

"I'm happy," he said, his lips pressing into a flat line like his heartbeat. "So fucking happy."

"I thought you liked living in the bayou. Someone piss you off?" Maurice slipped an arm around Amelie and dropped a kiss on her temple.

"No. I'm just wondering if I really belong here. I'm thinking of maybe transferring to the Colorado region or Hawaii. Hell, I might as well go back on active duty."

"You have friends here. You're part of the team. We're brothers, man."

"What team?" he muttered. "Most of you guys go home to your wives or significant others. I go home to my empty house. I've binge-watched every series known to man. I work out seven days a week. It's not enough. I need a change."

Amelie leaned around Maurice. "You need a girl."

In the back of his mind, he knew this. The fuck if he'd admit it to his friends. "I don't need anyone. I just need a change."

Maurice lifted his chin toward the pavilion. "Why not join the party? You might meet a woman there."

"That's not going to fix everything. I'm just not happy here."

"When was the last time you asked a woman out on a date?" Amelie asked.

"I don't know. Six months. A year ago." Xavier shrugged. "I think I know every woman in town. Either they aren't interested, or I'm not."

"Then mingle with the tourists. Ask one of them out," Maurice said.

As they'd walked, they'd arrived at the square. People were laughing, dancing and eating Cajun food.

"I see Gisele," Amelie said. "I had a question for her. You two enjoy the fun—but not too much fun." She hurried off to find her friend, leaving Maurice stuck with him.

"Why don't you strike up a conversation with that one?" Maurice lifted his chin toward a woman wearing a leopard-print halter-top with short jean shorts and cowboy boots.

"No," Xavier said.

"There's a pretty one in pink," Maurice continued.

"No."

"How about her? The one in the flowy psychedelic dress and the long straight black hair. She's pretty." Maurice squinted. "No, wait. That's Lissette Gautier. She might be more than you can handle. She's known to stir up trouble and break hearts." He turned away. "Moving on."

Xavier tuned out Maurice as his gaze followed Lissette in her crazy colored dress. On some women, it would look outlandish. On Lissette...? It suited her. Afterall, she was the granddaughter of Bayou Mambaloa's Voodoo Queen.

Lisette was flirting with a man, batting her eyes and laughing. Her face lit up in the lights.

He'd seen her around town and run into her at the Crawdad Hole a few times and hadn't given her a second thought.

Maybe she was what he needed to shake the boredom out of him.

As he started toward her, she walked away with the man, leaning on his arm.

Xavier sighed. He spent the next fifteen minutes wandering through the crowd, just not feeling it. He decided he might as well go home.

As he walked back down Main Street, he toyed with the idea of getting a dog. They were good companions. They loved unconditionally and didn't hog the bathroom in the morning.

He'd just about convinced himself it was a good idea when he heard a scream.

His pulse quickened as he looked around for the source of the scream.

Another scream ripped through the air. It seemed to be coming from the alley between the insurance office and the yoga studio. He ran that direction and had just reached the entry to the alley when a woman ran out and plowed into him.

He wrapped his arms around her to steady her. "Hey, hey. I've got you. You're safe. Are you all right? Did someone hurt you?"

"Yes. He slapped me," she said, and looked up into his face with deep, dark eyes like pools of indigo. Her long black hair fell straight down her back in inky waves, and the flowy dress she wore lifted in the breeze like wings on a butterfly. "Thank you," she said. "I think you scared him away."

"You're Lizette Guatier, aren't you? The Voodoo Queen's granddaughter?"

She nodded. "And you're one of those Brotherhood Protectors Remy brought in a couple of years ago."

He nodded. "I'm Xavier, Xander if you prefer. Nice to formally meet you."

She studied him with a tilt of her chin. "You're not afraid of being with me?"

"Should I be?" he asked.

"Most people warn men about me. They say I'm trouble." She straightened her dress and stepped away from him. "Look, you seem like a nice guy. You should listen to those warnings. I'm not for the likes of you. Go home. Pet your dog. Find a nice girl to date."

Lissette touched a hand to his cheek. "Such a shame. You're kind of cute." She leaned up, pressed her lips to his, then turned and walked away.

Xavier watched her hips sway, swooshing the dress around her ankles, and thought that his life might just have gotten interesting.

Waving a warning in his face was like flapping a cape at a bull.

Challenge accepted.

.   .   .

THANK YOU FOR READING MAURICE. The Bayou Brotherhood Protectors Series continues with Xavier

INTERESTED IN MORE MILITARY romance stories? Subscribe to my newsletter and receive the Military Heroes Box Set

Subscribe Here

CHILLED

A KILLER SERIES BOOK #1

New York Times & *USA Today*
Bestselling Author

ELLE JAMES

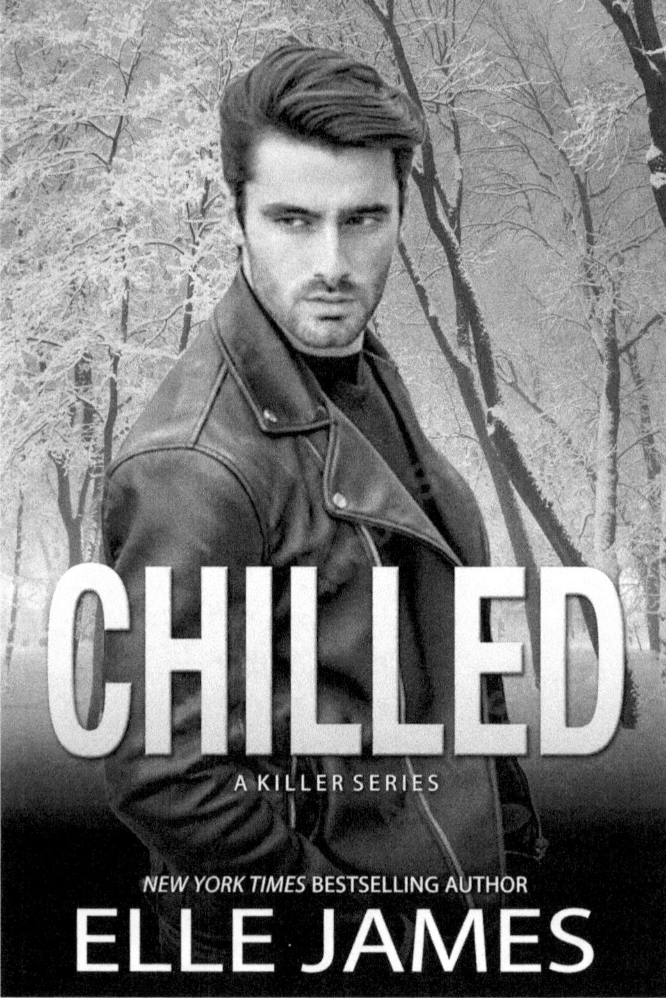

CHILLED
A KILLER SERIES
NEW YORK TIMES BESTSELLING AUTHOR
ELLE JAMES

CHAPTER 1

THE KILLING's only just begun. Watch them drop now, one by one.

FOR THE PAST seven hours the words echoed through Brenna's head. No amount of loud music or talking to herself erased the sound, repeating like a mantra again and again.

When she finally slid her Jeep Cherokee into the driveway of the police station and parked on a hump of ice, she sat for a moment, letting the heater blow warm air in her face. If she had any strength left in her arms after the grueling drive, she would shake a fist at the sky.

Yesterday, she'd been fooled into believing spring had arrived with sunshine melting through the mounds of solid ice piled four feet deep outside her townhouse in Bismarck.

With a sigh, she switched off the engine, pulled her gloves on and wrapped a wool scarf around her face before she stepped out into the storm. The storm that had raged since midnight had dipped its sub-zero blast as far south as Des Moines.

A native of the northern prairie, she knew better than to count on spring arriving any sooner than April and usually not until May. Her eyes stung, and she pulled her scarf higher over her nose to ward off the bite of the icy wind. Still wired by her hair-raising drive from Bismarck in whiteout conditions, Brenna stomped loose snow from her insulated boots outside the door to the Riverton Police Station.

The weatherman had predicted snow flurries. However, one thing North Dakotans could count on was the unpredictable, harsh weather. A trip that usually took her three and a half hours had taken twice as long at half the speed.

In any other circumstance, she'd have waited to make the trip until the storm had passed and the road crew had worked its magic, clearing away the foot of snow already accumulated. The forty-mile-an-hour wind hadn't helped either. She'd struggled to see the road through the heavy snowfall and fought the gale-force gusts buffeting her four-wheel-drive vehicle all over the interstate highway. But she'd made it.

Stepping through the two sets of doors, Brenna entered the police station. The reviving scent of brewing coffee filled her senses as she divested herself of the scarf and draped it over a hook, followed by gloves, stocking cap and, finally, her heavy parka. Even the short walk from her car to the building necessitated full snow gear unless she wanted frostbite. The coffee smelled even better without the wool filter around her nose, and she yearned to wrap her stiff fingers around a hot cup. But first, she needed to find Tom.

She planted her hands on the counter and leaned toward the curious young police officer. "Hi, I'm Brenna Jensen. Where can I find Chief Burkholder?"

"That you, Brenna?" a deep voice called out from a doorway beyond the front desk.

Her smile lifted upward as her mentor and old friend Chief Tom Burkholder stepped into the lobby.

When she held out her hand to shake his, he brushed it aside and engulfed her in a bear hug that forced the air from her lungs. God, it felt good to be home, even in such tragic circumstances.

Chief Burkholder set her away from him and stared down at her face. "Did you stop by to see your mother and sister yet?"

"Are you kidding?" She tipped her head to the side and back to loosen the muscles tensed in her shoulders and neck. "As soon as they assigned me to the case, I headed straight here."

"You're just like your father—all about the job. We sure miss him around here."

Her father had died of a massive heart attack two years after Brenna had joined the Riverton Police Department. He'd been so proud of his daughters' accomplishments, especially when Brenna had chosen to follow in his footsteps. Never once had he bemoaned the fact he hadn't had a son.

She missed her father. They'd understood each other, and he'd loved her unconditionally.

"Heard you're up for a new job in Minneapolis," the chief said.

"Yeah." A twinge of guilt nudged at Brenna, as if leaving North Dakota was the equivalent of a sin, when so many young people fled the state to find jobs. In her case, she had a job, but the new one meant an increase in pay and responsibility, with the downside of being farther away from her family.

"When do they make the final selection?" Tom asked.

"In a week and a half."

"I'll keep you in my prayers for the job and this case." He hugged her again. "You deserve the break." The chief dropped his hands, shoved them in his pocket and stared down at his feet. "In the meantime, things been happenin' around here."

"Did you find the women?" Brenna asked.

The chief shook his head, his skin almost as gray as his hair. "No. We had dozens of state police and local citizens combing the countryside all weekend, but the storm...well, *you* know what it was like. We pulled them in as soon as the weather got bad. No use losing anyone else in that mess out there."

"Find anything in the victims' homes?"

"Nothing yet. Only thing we got to go on is—"

"—what the good ol' U.S. Post Office delivered directly to me," Brenna finished for him. Her mouth set in a bleak line. "I don't know what to make of it, but I sure as hell plan to find out."

"One other thing..." Chief Burkholder tugged at the tie already loose around his neck.

Brenna recognized the signs. Chief had more bad news he didn't want to tell her.

Her lips twisted into a faux smile, and she patted his back. "Might as well spit it out."

With a shake of his head, Chief Burkholder stared hard at her. "We had another woman from town go missing last night."

As if a heavy clamp pinched her lungs, Brenna fought to breathe normally. "Then the note is coming true. You sure she didn't go somewhere and forget to tell anyone?"

"No. Her car was still in her garage, her purse on the counter in the kitchen." The chief chewed on his lower lip. "And, Brenna, since victim number two was from East Riverton on the Minnesota side of the Red River, we notified the FBI. They're taking charge of the investigation."

"Great. Let's hope they don't hamper our search like the last team they sent." She walked toward the coffee urn on the side counter and helped herself to a foam cup full of liquid resembling sludge. "I'm beginning to see what ol' Red McClusky meant when he said, 'We don't need no outsiders muckin' around our neck of the woods.' I just hope the hell they don't slow us down."

"I'm sorry you feel that way." A low, rumbling voice sounded over Brenna's left shoulder.

She froze. Then a wave of heat rose from beneath her turtleneck to fan out into her face.

Inhaling deeply, she steeled her nerves and willed her cheeks to quit burning before she faced the voice. "Do you always sneak up on private conversations?"

"Only if it has something to do with the case I'm working." The man in front of her could have stepped out of an ad for an action-adventure cop movie. In his black leather jacket, black hair falling across his forehead, and eyes an intense emerald-green, he was too perfect to be true. The addition of a five-o'clock shadow only made him look better—a perfect male specimen, from a scientific viewpoint.

Science be damned. Brenna didn't need a perfect man making a mess out of this case. She didn't need distractions when women were being kidnapped and more than likely murdered in her hometown.

"Nick Tarver." He held out his hand without smiling or baring his teeth to soften the sharp lines of his face, only those intense eyes staring straight into hers. "I'd hoped for an amicable relationship with the locals while working this case."

"Special Agent Brenna Jensen, North Dakota Bureau of Criminal Investigations." *Not nice to meet you*, she added without voicing the sentiment. Maybe she was a bit touchy about the subject, but she didn't need another case screwed up by the FBI, or another physically faultless person in her life. Having her sister and her sister's husband thrown in her face at every chance her mother could get was already enough to make her want to scream. Why couldn't the FBI send a really ugly, capable agent instead of Nick Tarver?

As Nick shook her hand, he observed the way Brenna Jensen's forehead settled into a permanent frown. Instead of making her less attractive, she appeared like a fierce kitten ready to pounce on a wolf. And he was the wolf. He almost laughed until a pang of awareness registered in his libido.

This woman, who barely came up to his shoulder, with her straight sandy-blond hair and blue eyes, was like the girl next door. Fresh, clean and wholesome. Too small and vulnerable to be a cop. She was the kind of girl a guy could take home to meet his mother. Someone he might have liked knowing, if he hadn't already sworn off women. And as a potential victim, Brenna Jensen presented more of a liability than an asset to his case.

"Mind if I keep that?" She glanced down at the hand he still held and back up at him, her brows rising. "I'm sort of attached to it."

He jerked his hand away and stepped back, for a moment off balance and not liking it.

Brenna tipped her head toward the doorway leading to the rear of the building. "Show me where you're set up, and I'll show you my note."

"Not yet."

Her shoulders straightened, and she dragged in a deep, slow breath, as if preparing to go into battle. "What do you mean, not yet?"

"Before we do anything else, we need your statement."

The woman let the air out of her lungs. "On one condition…"

Tarver's brows dipped into a frown. He wasn't used to negotiating his orders. He opened his mouth to say so, but Brenna beat him to it.

"I keep my coffee." She gave him a saccharine-sweet smile.

His brows met in the middle before they straightened, and he nodded. She'd better not push him. He'd have her out of the building so fast—

Coffee in hand, she sailed toward the door leading into the back of the police station.

He hurried to follow her, falling in step behind her.

Before she'd gone too far down the hallway, she stopped so abruptly Nick bumped into her. Her body was soft and feminine, but beneath the layers of clothing, he could feel the steely strength of well-honed muscles.

Her mouth made a small O and then firmed into a straight line as she looked over his shoulder to the man behind him. "Interview room still in the same place, Chief?"

"You betcha," Tom Burkholder replied.

"Let's go, Tarver." With a dismissive glance, she resumed her pace.

"Nick. Call me Nick." He almost smiled at the cocky little she-devil's back. He preferred a woman with spunk—but not at work. At work, he liked people to follow orders. "Chief Burkholder will take your statement."

"Whatever. Let's get this interview over so we can get to work solving this case."

He stepped around her and led the way through a bank of desks to a room located near the rear of the building. He held the door as the chief entered and Brenna followed. As she passed close enough to touch him, Nick caught the scents of herbal shampoo and fresh snow.

A strange combination of winter and spring. The unbidden impression formed in his mind from just that little whiff, and he brushed it aside.

That was too much detail about a witness he had no intention of keeping on his team.

Once they were inside the interview room, Nick Tarver closed the door, shutting them in and him out. He moved down the hall and stepped into the observation room to watch and listen to the interview through the two-way mirror.

Stark and plain, the room was basically empty, with only a heavy metal table and two folding chairs in the middle of the floor. A single, uncovered light bulb provided enough light to illuminate all four corners.

Brenna circled the room and stopped to stare into the mirror. "Hey, Agent Tarver, can you hear me? Because I don't want to repeat myself later."

He fought a sudden urge to chuckle. The woman was annoying, but ballsy.

Chief Burkholder waved toward a chair. "Have a seat, Special Agent Jensen." Gone was the surrogate-father figure, and in its place was the professional police officer.

She set her satchel on the floor and pulled out a photocopy of the note she'd received. "I suppose you'd like to see the copy of the note and the envelope…?"

He took the paper and shot a brief glance at it

before setting it to one side of the table. "Let's start at the beginning. Your full name."

"You know me, Chief." She glared at the mirror, her fingers tapping a rhythm on the tabletop.

She was impatient and possibly a bit nervous knowing Nick was watching her. He sat in a chair and crossed his arms over his chest. Good. Make her sweat. He was glad he'd chosen to watch instead of interrogating. This way he could study her openly.

The chief's lips twisted in a wry grin. "For the record, please. You know the drill."

With a sigh, she quit staring at the mirrored wall and stated, "Brenna Louise Jensen."

"Occupation—Special Agent for the North Dakota Bureau of Criminal Investigations?" the chief offered.

"That's right." She shot a defiant look at the mirror.

So, she was a criminal investigator. It didn't mean she'd work with him.

The older man wrote on a tablet and then looked up at her. "Tell me what happened."

"I found this letter in the mailbox at my townhouse when I got home from work on Friday."

Chief Burkholder sat up straight, his pen poised in midair. "Not at work, but at home?"

Nick leaned forward. That was news. He'd assumed she'd gotten it at her office. This meant the kidnapper knew where she lived.

She nodded. "Right."

"And there were no prints?" They knew there weren't any, but the chief had to put it into the record.

"No."

"Where was the letter postmarked?" the chief asked.

"Riverton Post Office." She sighed. "That's why I'm here."

"In your line of work, have you been assigned to cases involving violent criminals?"

Her chin rose as if challenging the man behind the wall. "Yeah. That's my job."

The chief scribbled her answers on the notepad before he looked up again. "And Riverton's your hometown, isn't it?"

"Yes, sir," she stated. "It's where I grew up."

The chief continued. "Has anyone from Riverton ever threatened you?"

"No," she said, her fingers drumming against the tabletop again.

"Were you ever involved in an incident that would make someone consider you a threat?"

Her hand stilled. "Other than my case work?"

"Correct."

She hesitated, darting another glance at the mirror as she tucked a long strand of hair behind her ear. "No."

Was the hair flicking a nervous gesture? Was she not telling the chief something? Nick's gut said yes. What secrets could a criminal investigator have?

Chief Burkholder continued the questioning without delving into her answer. If Nick had conducted the interview, he'd have questioned her further. But she was a cop and probably didn't think the information was relevant to the case.

When the interview was over, Brenna stood and gathered her satchel and the copy of her note. "Now can we get on with solving this case?"

"Eager, aren't we?" The chief patted her shoulder. "Come on, I'll show you where they've set up."

Nick left the observation room ahead of Brenna and the chief and beat them to the large conference room. It had been converted to a "war room." Completely covering one wall was a large whiteboard with a timeline sketched out in black erasable marker. Three notches were marked with the names of the missing women and the times they'd been reported missing. Another spot was marked "Note."

Now that he had Brenna's statement, she wasn't necessary to the case, and Nick wanted her out of the station and on her way back to Bismarck.

Although she was another key to solving the case, Nick had no intention of allowing her onto his team. He liked to work with people he knew and trusted. Get in, solve the crime, get out and don't get involved. That was Nick's policy, and he sure as hell didn't want to be in this godforsaken, frigid country any longer than he had to. He braced himself for the coming clash of wills with Special Agent Jensen.

The woman topmost on his mind breezed into the war room and tossed her satchel onto the conference table as if throwing down the gauntlet.

Chief Burkholder handed Nick the copy of the note he'd already seen as a blurry faxed copy they'd received around four that morning while Jensen had been in route.

Nick laid the paper on the table and walked over to Brenna. No time like the present. "Thank you for your statement, Special Agent Jensen. We no longer need your services. I advise you to return to Bismarck and lock your doors."

She stared up into his face for a long moment, her rate of breathing increasing until the air she exhaled blew in a sharp stream out her nose. Then she stepped closer to him, until her chest bumped against his. "I'm an experienced investigator assigned to this case by the state of North Dakota. I'm not running from some jerk who thinks he can pull my chain."

"Agent Tarver," Chief Burkholder said and then cleared his throat. "Jensen is one of North Dakota's best."

"I don't care." Tarver's eyes never left her face, and his expression remained unflinching. "She's a liability. I can't focus on the case if I'm playing bodyguard."

Her face flushed red. "I don't need your protection. I've been in law enforcement for six years. I can take care of myself."

That she hadn't backed down impressed him at the same time it annoyed him. "In case you haven't gotten the picture, the FBI has jurisdiction and is calling the shots now. You're off the case."

"Understand this, Agent Tarver. I *will* be involved fully in this case, with or without the FBI. I have more at stake here than you or any of your agents. This is my hometown, not yours. Nobody gets away with kidnapping or murder in my hometown."

"Agent Tarver, Special Agent Jensen was assigned from the state level. She won't be returning to Bismarck. If you don't include her on the team, she'll work alone to solve this case. You'd better serve the cause by including her." Chief Burkholder laid a hand on Nick's shoulder.

Okay, so the girl had the chief's confidence. He could admire that, but he didn't like being forced to accept her on his team. He shook off the chief's hand and stared down his nose into Brenna's clear blue eyes. "Get this straight, Jensen, I give the orders. Do you understand?"

For a moment, he thought she'd spit in his eye and tell him to go to hell. But her shoulders pushed back, and she met his gaze head-on. "I do."

"Good. Then don't get in my way."

"So does that mean I'm a part of the team?"

"I'll let you know." For a moment, Nick swam in the depths of her stormy blue eyes—until he remembered how badly he'd been burned by a woman with blue eyes and why he'd never go there again. "Time's wasting. We've got a killer to catch before he does it again."

Read more of CHILLED.

ABOUT THE AUTHOR

ELLE JAMES also writing as MYLA JACKSON is a *New York Times* and *USA Today* Bestselling author of books including cowboys, intrigues and paranormal adventures that keep her readers on the edges of their seats. When she's not at her computer, she's traveling, snow skiing, boating, or riding her ATV, dreaming up new stories. Learn more about Elle James at www.ellejames.com

Website | Facebook | Twitter | GoodReads | Newsletter | BookBub | Amazon

Or visit her alter ego Myla Jackson at mylajackson.com
Website | Facebook | Twitter | Newsletter

Follow Me!
www.ellejames.com
ellejamesauthor@gmail.com

Stealth Operations Specialists Series

Saint Nick (#1)

Rogue (#2)

Crusher (#3)

Draco (#4)

A Killer Series

Chilled (#1)

Scorched (#2)

Erased (#3)

Brotherhood Protectors International

Athens Affair (#1)

Belgian Betrayal (#2)

Croatia Collateral (#3)

Dublin Debacle (#4)

Edinburgh Escape (#5)

France Face-Off (#6)

Brotherhood Protectors Hawaii

Kalea's Hero (#1)

Leilani's Hero (#2)

Kiana's Hero (#3)

Casey's Hero (#4)

Maliea's Hero (#5)

Emi's Hero (#6)

Sachie's Hero (#7)

Kimo's Hero (#8)

Alana's Hero (#9)

Bayou Brotherhood Protectors

Remy (#1)

Gerard (#2)

Lucas (#3)

Beau (#4)

Rafael (#5)

Valentin (#6)

Landry (#7)

Simon (#8)

Maurice (#9)

Xavier (#10)

Jacques (#11)

Papa Noel (#12)

Everglades Overwatch Series

with Jen Talty

Secrets in Calusa Cove

Pirates in Calusa Cove

Murder in Calusa Cove

Betrayal in Calusa Cove

Raven's Cliff Series

with Kris Norris

Raven's Watch (#1)

Raven's Claw (#2)

Raven's Nest (#3)

Raven's Curse (#4)

Brotherhood Protectors Yellowstone

Saving Kyla (#1)

Saving Chelsea (#2)

Saving Amanda (#3)

Saving Liliana (#4)

Saving Breely (#5)

Saving Savvie (#6)

Saving Jenna (#7)

Saving Peyton (#8)

Saving Londyn (#9)

Brotherhood Protectors Colorado

SEAL Salvation (#1)

Rocky Mountain Rescue (#2)

Ranger Redemption (#3)

Tactical Takeover (#4)

Colorado Conspiracy (#5)

Rocky Mountain Madness (#6)

Free Fall (#7)

Colorado Cold Case (#8)

Fool's Folly (#9)

Colorado Free Rein (#10)

Rocky Mountain Venom (#11)

High Country Hero (#12)

Brotherhood Protectors

Montana SEAL (#1)

Bride Protector SEAL (#2)

Montana D-Force (#3)

Cowboy D-Force (#4)

Montana Ranger (#5)

Montana Dog Soldier (#6)

Montana SEAL Daddy (#7)

Montana Ranger's Wedding Vow (#8)

Montana SEAL Undercover Daddy (#9)

Cape Cod SEAL Rescue (#10)

Montana SEAL Friendly Fire (#11)

Montana SEAL's Mail-Order Bride (#12)

SEAL Justice (#13)

Ranger Creed (#14)

Delta Force Rescue (#15)

Dog Days of Christmas (#16)

Montana Rescue (#17)

Montana Ranger Returns (#18)

Brotherhood Protectors Boxed Set 1

Brotherhood Protectors Boxed Set 2

Brotherhood Protectors Boxed Set 3

Brotherhood Protectors Boxed Set 4

Brotherhood Protectors Boxed Set 5

Brotherhood Protectors Boxed Set 6

Iron Horse Legacy

Soldier's Duty (#1)

Ranger's Baby (#2)

Marine's Promise (#3)

SEAL's Vow (#4)

Warrior's Resolve (#5)

Drake (#6)

Grimm (#7)

Murdock (#8)

Utah (#9)

Judge (#10)

Delta Force Strong

Ivy's Delta (Delta Force 3 Crossover)

Breaking Silence (#1)

Breaking Rules (#2)

Breaking Away (#3)

Breaking Free (#4)

Breaking Hearts (#5)

Breaking Ties (#6)

Breaking Point (#7)

Breaking Dawn (#8)

Breaking Promises (#9)

Hearts & Heroes Series

Wyatt's War (#1)

Mack's Witness (#2)

Ronin's Return (#3)

Sam's Surrender (#4)

Hellfire Series

Hellfire, Texas (#1)

Justice Burning (#2)

Smoldering Desire (#3)

Hellfire in High Heels (#4)

Playing With Fire (#5)

Up in Flames (#6)

Total Meltdown (#7)

Take No Prisoners Series

SEAL's Honor (#1)

SEAL'S Desire (#2)

SEAL's Embrace (#3)

SEAL's Obsession (#4)

SEAL's Proposal (#5)

SEAL's Seduction (#6)

SEAL'S Defiance (#7)

SEAL's Deception (#8)

SEAL's Deliverance (#9)

SEAL's Ultimate Challenge (#10)

Cajun Magic Mystery Series

Voodoo on the Bayou (#1)

Voodoo for Two (#2)

Deja Voodoo (#3)

Texas Billionaire Club

Tarzan & Janine (#1)

Something To Talk About (#2)

Who's Your Daddy (#3)

Love & War (#4)

Billionaire Online Dating Service

The Billionaire Husband Test (#1)

The Billionaire Cinderella Test (#2)

The Billionaire Bride Test (#3)

The Billionaire Daddy Test (#4)

The Billionaire Matchmaker Test (#5)

The Billionaire Glitch Date (#6)

The Outriders

Homicide at Whiskey Gulch (#1)

Hideout at Whiskey Gulch (#2)

Held Hostage at Whiskey Gulch (#3)

Setup at Whiskey Gulch (#4)

Missing Witness at Whiskey Gulch (#5)

Cowboy Justice at Whiskey Gulch (#6)

Boys Behaving Badly Anthologies

Rogues (#1)

Blue Collar (#2)

Pirates (#3)

Stranded (#4)

First Responder (#5)

Cowboys (#6)

Silver Soldiers (#7)

Secret Identities (#8)

Warrior's Conquest

Enslaved by the Viking Short Story

Conquests

Smokin' Hot Firemen

Protecting the Colton Bride

Protecting the Colton Bride & Colton's Cowboy Code

Heir to Murder

Secret Service Rescue

High Octane Heroes

Haunted

Engaged with the Boss

Cowboy Brigade

An Unexpected Clue

Under Suspicion, With Child

Texas-Size Secrets

9 781626 956735